IN THE SERVICE
OF DRAGONS III

BOOK THREE

ROBERT STANEK

In the Service of Dragons III

Copyright © 2005 by Robert Stanek.

First Edition, August 2005

All rights reserved, including the right to reproduce this book, or portions thereof, in any form. Printed in the United States of America.

Reagent Press

Published by Virtual Press, Inc.

Cover design & illustration by Robert Stanek

Cover illustration copyright © 2005 Robert Stanek

Inside illustration copyright © 2005 Reagent Press

ISBN 1-57545-093-3

REAGENT PRESS

Reagent Press Books by Robert Stanek

Keeper Martin's Tales
The Kingdoms & the Elves of the Reaches, Book 1
The Kingdoms & the Elves of the Reaches II, Book 2
The Kingdoms & the Elves of the Reaches III, Book 3
The Kingdoms & the Elves of the Reaches IV, Book 4
In the Service of Dragons, Book 5
In the Service of Dragons II, Book 6
In the Service of Dragons III, Book 7
In the Service of Dragons IV, Book 8

Ruin Mist Tales
The Elf Queen & the King, Book 1
The Elf Queen & the King II, Book 2
The Elf Queen & the King III, Book 3
The Elf Queen & the King IV, Book 4

Ruin Mist Heroes, Legends & Beyond
Magic of Ruin Mist

Magic Lands
Journey Beyond the Beyond
Into the Stone Land

Magic Lands & Other Stories

Praise for Ruin Mist & Keeper Martin's Tales

"A gem waiting to be unearthed by millions of fans of fantasy!"

"Brilliant… an absolutely superior tale of fantasy for all tastes!"

"It's a creative, provoking, and above all, thoughtful story!"

"It's a wonderful metaphor for the dark (and light) odyssey of the mind."

"The fantasy world you have created is truly wonderful and rich. Your characters seem real and full of life."

Learn more at www.robertstanek.com

Enter the world of the books
www.ruinmist.com

Meet the Characters

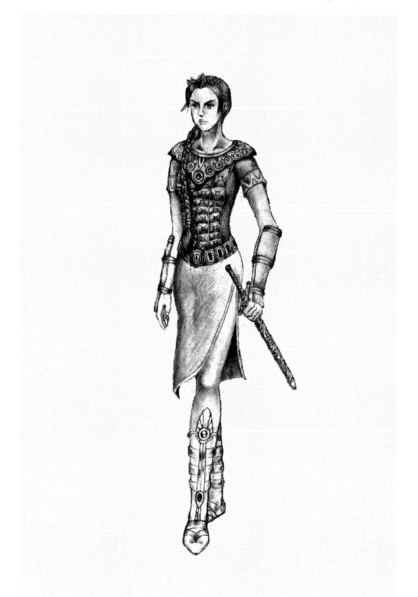

Adrina Alder
Princess Adrina. Third and youngest
daughter of King Andrew.

Amir
Son of Ky'el,
King of the Titans.

Ansh Brodst
Captain Brodst.
King's Knight Captain.

Cagan
Sailmaster Cagan.
Elven ship captain.

Calyin Alder
Princess Calyin.
Eldest daughter of King Andrew.

Delinna Alder
Known as Sister Midori after joining
the priestesses.

Jacob Froen d'Ga
Father Jacob. First minister to the
King. Head of the priesthood in Imtal.

Jarom Tyr'anth
King Jarom, ruler of Vostok,
East Warden of the Word.

Liyan
Brother Liyan. Presiding member of
East Reach High Council.

Mark
King Mark. The Elven King of West Reach.

Martin Braddabaggon
Keeper Martin. A lore Keeper and
head of the Council of Keepers.

Noman
Keeper of the City of the Sky.

Queen Mother
The Elven Queen of East Reach.

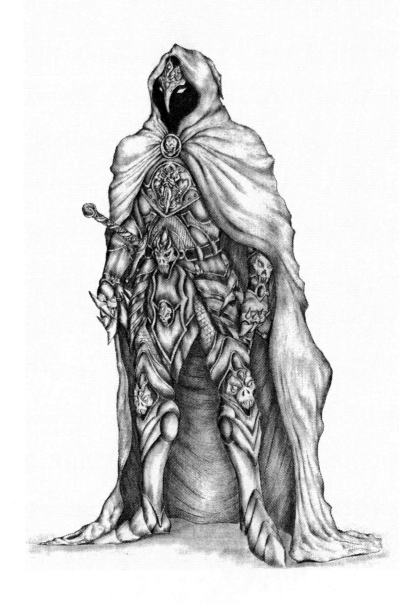

Sathar
The dark lord.

Seth
Elf, first of the Red,
protector of Queen Mother.

Tsandra
First of the Brown.

Vadan Evgej
Captain Evgej. Former Swordmaster,
city garrison at Quashan'.

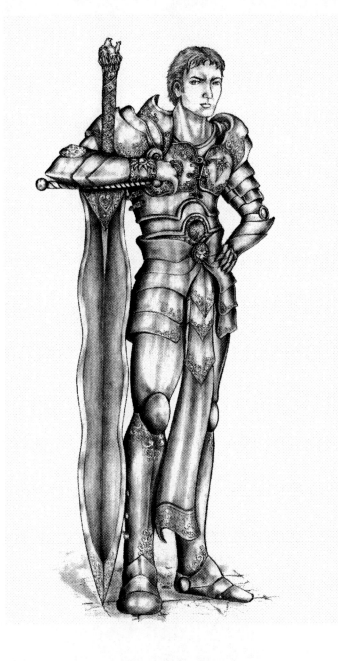

Valam Alder
Prince Valam. Only son of King
Andrew.

Vilmos Tabborrath
An apprentice of the forbidden arcane arts.

Xith
Last of the Watchers.

Where the Story Ended Last Time

Princess Calyin's face blanched as the words fell heavily upon her. "What is this outrage?" she cried out. "I will not have it! There will be no test!"

Father Joshua put his hands gently on Calyin's shoulders and attempted to calm her down. Calyin would not calm her tongue for anyone. She pushed Father Joshua aside and rose from her seat. Her face was now dark with anger. Calyin, with eyes cold and fixed, glared around the room, daring anyone to say anything further on the subject. No one with was willing to challenge her, so all remained quiet for a time.

King Jarom, heavily endowed with shrewdness but lacking the better graces of wisdom and good judgment, broke the silence, "Princess Calyin, know your place and calm your tongue!"

"Calm my tongue? I will hold my tongue when I am good and ready to do so; however, until then I will continue to speak my mind! It is you who needs to gain your bearing and remember your place. You are not in your tiny little kingdom any more! You are in my kingdom! In my palace! And furthermore, you are a guest! A guest should know his place!" screamed Calyin as she stalked across the room to confront Jarom face to face.

As she approached, King Jarom's air of superiority modified to become a small, trembling ember, which Calyin devoured. "I demand a recount now! And by the same treatise that brought us here, I am allowed to call for a new count! If there is anyone who disagrees, let him speak!"

Calyin stormed back across the hall and sat down. King Jarom, with a shocked expression on his face, quietly retook his position. Lord Serant, controlling his desire to smile, quickly seated himself beside Calyin.

Chancellor Volnej quelled the growing disorder in the hall. Harshly, he cleared his throat and thumped his scepter several more times to silence the last few murmurs. "It is thus written. A recount is in order. We will pause for a turning of the glass, then begin."

Lord Serant turned to Calyin and smiled with amazement. As their time together grew, he felt his love for her grow with each passing year. He needed her more than she would ever know.

All attention turned back to the rear of the hall where the counting would start. Talem stood and made a symbolic gesture with his hands. The other dark priests rose as one and together they intoned a definitive no. Keeper Q'yer smiled and intoned a triumphant yes. Father Joshua and Sister Midori each again affirmed a yes.

Calyin stood and turned to look into the tiers. Keeper Q'yer followed her move, also rising; the other keepers were quick to follow suit. Each individual counselor offered an unequivocal yes and with pride remained standing in salutation. Geoffrey, Lord Fantyu, Chancellor Van'te, and King William completed the movement. The other votes were of no consequence. The vote was clearly changed. Lord Serant would be magistrate for as long as he deemed necessary. Angrily, Chancellor de Vit penned his signature onto the new document Volnej gave him. The vote became fact as the scroll was passed to Chancellor Van'te for his confirmation; there would be no debate this time. The decision was no longer a draw.

"My dear, dear, Princess Calyin. These little games of state do bore me so," haughtily stated King Jarom, "but I wish to thank you very much. You don't know how much I am in your debt."

Awed silence befell upon the hall. King Jarom's crafty smirk widened as tension filled the air. Keeper Q'yer raised his hands to his temples. The intensity of his headache was unbearable. It was as he did this mechanically without thought that he realized something peculiar. The pain of the headache had been as a cloud over his thoughts, but until just now he hadn't noticed it. However, in the back of his thoughts he knew he had been feeling ill since early morning.

His eyes nervously wandered about the chamber. He noted that Father Joshua also looked rather pale. His thoughts began to run wild; he could not concentrate. The pain within his mind was growing, becoming unbearable. He just wanted to rip it out and throw it away.

The keeper strained to clear his mind. Time seemed to be flowing so quickly. He shouted out, "Oh the pain, the pain, it will not go!" but the words never left his mind.

With a snap of his fingers, King Jarom ended the calm. The holy seal on the great doors splintered and fell to the floor. A faint battering noise resounded from somewhere beyond the chamber, followed momentarily by the stifling sound of the crash. The double doors of the room burst open and fell heavily.

A torrent of heavily armored soldiers shouted a gallant cheer and poured into the chamber. In that instant, Keeper Q'yer crumpled unconscious over the table in front of him. Thought returned to him momentarily as he fell; he knew without a doubt that the beginning of the end had begun.

Shock and disbelief paralyzed the gathered throng. The hall was in turmoil even before the enemy warriors stormed into the room. Father Joshua felt with bitterness the anguish in Keeper Q'yer's spirit as it passed. The pain outside his consciousness allowed him to wrench his mind away from the enchantment of the agony within, and thought returned to him.

The dark priests released a mocking laugh as their energies revived. Their mental strength spent beyond their capacities, they could not withstand the impact. The priests had completed their task to perfection, so they gladly did the only thing they could do—they expired. Save one, who sought to flee the turmoil in the chamber.

Lord Serant sprang from his chair and readied for the coming battle. He cleared his mind and prepared for the fight. He would make the traitors pay dearly for this treachery. Once his thoughts were organized, his first duty was to try to get Calyin to safety. Rapidly he assessed the situation.

Jarom had been thorough in his planning; the hall was as an

erupting volcano of melee. Lord Serant was grateful that he had foreseen something coming although the treachery had not come directly from Chancellor Volnej as he had expected. He scanned the hall rapidly, searching for Pyetr to signal him to send for reinforcements.

The sentries posted throughout the chamber were quick to react to the danger, and were making a valiant effort to contain the invading horde. Their high-quality light mail gave them a clear advantage over the intruders, who were outfitted in heavy mail beneath large cloaks. Many of the enemies were wasting valuable time removing their guise; although it only took moments to remove the heavy cloaks, it was sufficient to end many of their lives. Their numbers were in no way hindered by the losses.

Captain Brodst grabbed Lord Serant by the tunic and ushered him and Princess Calyin into a far corner of the hall. Lord Serant was offended by the action, but his pride was not damaged. He knew the captain was just looking out for his safety.

Lord Serant cast an angry glare at Chancellor Volnej, who stood nervously beside Chancellor Van'te. The keepers without the leadership of Keeper Q'yer were beset by confusion. The keeper's demise had been sudden and unnerving. They still remained in the tiers along the side of the chamber.

Father Joshua quickly followed Talem, pursuing him into the mass of bodies set before the entryway without thought. He latched onto the dark priest's robe, pulling him backwards, and when the opportunity arose, he pummeled him to the ground. Without hesitation, Father Joshua struck Talem in the face, once for Keeper Q'yer and once for himself.

Their bodyguards, who would at all cost protect the lives of the ones they served, quickly surrounded Geoffrey and the governors of Mir and Veter. As free men, they did not fear melee; it was part of their daily lives. They lived and would die by the sword.

The end came.

Chapter One

With the death of Keeper Q'yer, the battle in the great hall began. Midori and Catrin were slow in recovering from the pain inside. Lord Fantyu, although close-by, was not quick enough to stop their assailants from reaching them. A mailed hand cuffed Catrin and knocked her backward. The large figure laughed as he watched her fall, tumbling down the tiered rows. He grabbed Midori by her long hair and pulled her close to him, close enough so she could feel his breath against her face, and the foulness of it revolted her.

The council members were in panic. They ran blindly toward the great doors, following each other to their deaths. Lord Serant could only watch as they were easily cut down, their blood running bright across the floor. His goal, as well as Captain Brodst's, was to get to safety with Calyin and anyone else who could follow. Although he did feel sorrow in his heart for the deaths of the others, he did not have time to wait for old men, and their end only made it easier for him to leave the chamber without regrets.

Lord Fantyu drew his sword and swiftly ran Midori's assailant through. The expression on the warrior's face went from shocked dismay to horror as he watched the tip of the blade thrust out of his abdomen. Lord Fantyu quickly withdrew his blade and delivered a slapping blow to an attacker that moved toward him from the side. His elbow was quick to follow, as was his sword. He grabbed Midori by the hand and pulled her away. "But Catrin?" she yelled.

Lord Fantyu ignored her words and retreated to the rear of the chamber, where Lord Serant and Captain Brodst had set up a defensive position. They had turned the long, oaken conference table onto its side and strewn the way with chairs piled high, standing at the ready, waiting for any aggressors to come their way.

Geoffrey watched and waited, conferring calmly with the two at his side. He pictured in his mind how the battle would unfold. He was unconcerned for his safety due to the presence of the four men who stood before him; he was absolutely confident of their ability to defend him.

Father Joshua withdrew his hand from Talem's face a third time and looked dead into the dark priest's eyes. "You will pay for your treachery!" he bellowed. Talem was by no account able to argue with him; his world spun before him, in dazzling shadings of black and white.

Lord Serant angrily glared around the hall. "Where was Pyetr? Damn it!" he cursed under his breath. His search stopped when he came upon the four kings, sitting relaxed in the same place they had occupied earlier. A very large contingent of guards was gathered around them, which did not move to join the fray. They stood at the ready with weapons waiting.

Lord Serant's eyes fell to the door that lay behind them; the ante-chamber was beyond. He wondered if they realized the door was there. He nudged Captain Brodst and carefully brought his attention to the door. Both realized what it meant, but they had no way to reach it.

The primary problem with that exit was the considerable number of foes they would have to engage to get to it; nevertheless, there were fewer men in the way of their escape in that direction, no matter how the two thought about it. The more Lord Serant pondered the possibility, the less he favored it. It was not worth the risk; there had to be another way.

The sentries, though outnumbered and overwhelmed, were holding their own. Of twenty, only ten remained. They watched with horror as the enemy continued to come at them in waves. Weapons danced in their hands with the sweat of their lives pouring into their every move. If they failed a block or parry, they were dead, and this they knew and understood very well.

"Damn it, Pyetr!" cursed Lord Serant aloud again. His heart raced with anxiety; his mind spun with possibilities, working through various plans of escape while his sword arm agitatedly held his weapon at his side. Anger and frustration suffused his face. He was forced to stand and watch and wait.

Similar thoughts were crossing Captain Brodst's mind. He too looked for any possible way to escape, and if luck befell him he would find a way past the kings' soldiers. For the first time, his attention moved to the keepers who still stood confused. The priests of the Father, who were not as quick to react as Father Joshua had been, stood directly adjacent to them.

Although he realized that they would be the next logical

target for the foe, he held no hopes of assisting them. He must keep his thoughts clear. He did not need the extra baggage. The priests could hold their own for a time; the Father would not easily relinquish their positions on this plane. The keepers, however, were as useless as the High Council had been. He saw a similar fate for them.

Strength of will returned to Midori as she shook off the last of the effects of the dark priests' powers over her. She could not believe she had fallen for their mind tricks. She could not believe what she saw. She clutched her ceremonial dagger firmly in her hand. Her eyes fixed clearly, precisely on the front of the chamber.

Thoughts now raged within her. She sought out Father Joshua, but he was nowhere to be found. She knew none of the other priests of the Father by name. She did not, however, let that distract her from her search among them for one that would suit her needs.

Her eyes went wide with excitement and anticipation. "Catrin," she reached out in thought. The Mother had truly smiled upon them. She saw life within Catrin; Catrin was alive.

A gasp of dismay came from Lord Serant's lips as he watched the last of the sentries fall. It became obvious to him who the leader of the attackers was as he watched the last few rounds of melee. He fixed a cold, icy stare upon the leader and waited for the moment when the attack would come. "Pyetr!" he screamed out in his mind, "Damn it, man, hurry!"

He sighed in relief as his eyes fell upon a small contingent that took a position between him and the intruders. Lord Fantyu had taken up a position there with his men. Nine stood defiantly waiting. Lord Fantyu offered him a reassuring nod; the attackers would have to come through him first.

An idea came to Lord Serant; he turned and glared at Chancellor Volnej. His hand swiftly, subconsciously brought his blade to the chancellor's throat. "This is all your doing! Is it not? You traitorous dog!" he yelled as he spit in the chancellor's face. "You are not worth killing! I should feed you to a pack of wolves and let the vultures pick at your carcass after they are finished!"

Chancellor Volnej swallowed harshly, his face registering confusion. He didn't understand what Lord Serant was saying—a traitor. He was no traitor. "What are you saying? Are you mad?"

Chancellor Van'te was also confused. "Lord Serant, you must be mistaken. I have known the chancellor for a number of years; there is no way he is a traitor. Our enemy lies out there, not here!"

Lord Serant was abashed and confused. "Chancellor Volnej is a traitor; I can prove it!" he stated, his voice quavering uncertainly.

"Lord Serant, please! I beg you, do not act foolishly. Think about what you are saying," begged Chancellor Van'te.

Chancellor Volnej said nothing further in his defense. The tip of Serant's blade at his throat that did not move was more than enough to hold his tongue. He did not want to infuriate the obviously stressed lord with even the slightest provocation.

Chapter Two

Prince Valam Alder departed Leklorall, capital city of East Reach, with few regrets. In his mind, he tried to understand all that happened since he went with Queen Mother to Shalan's tower. The tower that symbolized the heart and soul of the people of East Reach. The tower that only Queen Mother could enter—except that he had entered the tower and now the tower was no more.

He thought about the child of east and west, the bearer of light and remembrance. The one who was also the child of past and present, the bearer of darkness. The one who also hid the angel of life and the key. Was this his child or another?

The thought of having a child suddenly hit him. It was strange to think about. He, the lord and prince of the south, was to be a father. Would he be ready when the time came? Would he know what to do? Would the queen even let him see the child? Was she even with child? Was this so certain?

Soshi had told him once that she was with child but later said she had been mistaken. Thoughts of Soshi, his first true love, brought thoughts of the old blind woman who said she'd lost her sight for the greater good. "The old ways are all but forgotten now," the old woman had told him. "The old gods were not gods at all, merely creatures of power, great power." When she blinded him with the white powder, she said that she gave him a gift. It was Soshi though who took the blindness from him so that he might see truth.

He wished he could see truth now and he longed for Soshi's soothing ways though he knew he should not. Still, first love was an enduring love and his desire did not fade as the morning did. Later he could only picture Queen Mother's face in his mind's eye.

Seth strode up alongside Valam. "There, Valam, that is where the Eastern Plains begin," he said pointing to the line where the trees and the gentle sloping hills were replaced by the tall grasses and flatness of the plains. The plains stretched beyond the horizon into the distance. Its stark beauty was in its vastness and simplicity.

Valam's response was slow as he returned from his reverie. "It seems so endless."

"At times, I think it is."

"Yes, it has a beauty unique to itself," whispered Tsandra to Seth and Valam; she had walked up quietly behind them to look out over the vantage point. "Seth," she began, directing the thought only into his mind, "Please leave us for a moment." Seth didn't refuse her request; he smiled and returned to their small encampment.

"Valam, I haven't until now had an opportunity to properly beg your forgiveness. I do so now. Please forgive my shortsightedness. I acted without thought. I know it is something that is not easily forgotten, and even less easy to forgive, but I say this from within my very center. I am truly sorry."

Valam started to turn around to face her, but she stopped him. "No, please don't. I could not finish if you did."

"But I do not understand. You have done nothing to offend me."

"Shh, listen. I, most of all, should have known that you would do nothing to harm our queen intentionally. I betrayed your friendship, but what I can never forgive myself for was that I also acted out of jealousy. I—"

"What are you—jealous?"

"I know it is wrong, but I am in love with you."

"Love? What? Wait—stop a minute—say that again."

"I am sorry. I have said too much already. Come, we should go."

Brushing the tears from her eyes, Tsandra retreated from the hilltop, leaving Valam completely baffled. He watched her go; he wanted to scream at her but did not. He remained alone on top of the hill and tried to rethink his actions.

He watched as the others saddled their horses in preparation to rejoin the trail, then walked down the hill to join them. In minutes they were back in the saddle trotting toward the plains, leaving behind no signs that they had ever stopped here. They traversed the short distance to the grasslands quickly. It was almost instantaneous, as Valam crossed into the tall grasses, that he began to feel a peculiar sense grow within him.

His eyes began to search the plains rapidly back and forth. He had sensed this feeling once before though he could not place it.

His eyes followed down the line to Seth, Cagan, Evgej, Liyan, and finally Tsandra. Their eyes answered his unspoken question; they could also feel it.

With the passing of two days on the plain, the sensations only increased. The air began to grow colder and stronger, reaching sharply through their heavy riding clothes. Seth called a halt late in the afternoon. He held his hand up high, until the last of the group had formed and stopped.

"What's wrong?" asked Valam, wondering why they had stopped so soon. Seth pointed to a spot on the plains where the wind blew up dust in patches. A whisper of thought entered their minds. Valam had heard the sounds shallow within his mind before. He strained to concentrate only on listening. He could tell the sounds were words, but they were too weak to understand.

"I am Brother Seth, first of the order of the Red!" said Seth, reaching out with his mind. Valam perceived the thrust of Seth's energies like an explosion within his mind. He clenched his teeth tightly and immediately covered his ears. Evgej's reactions also brought his hands speedily to his ears. Although the action did nothing to curb the intensity of the burst of sound in their minds, it did appease their senses.

"Come! It is Brother Teren!" exclaimed Seth as he firmly swatted his steed with his tethers. The two groups of riders raced towards one another. It was not until the other group was in clear view that Valam realized that it was composed mainly of men. By the size and outfitting of the group, he estimated that it must be a scouting party, which Valam hoped to mean that the camp was close at hand.

"Supplies at last!" shouted Mikhal as he approached. He dropped to his feet quickly and knelt, with his head bowed in reverence. He did not allow the icy snow slapping his face to deter his moment of silence. "My prince, you live!" he shouted with a joyful voice, as he stood with his head still bowed.

Words fluttered to Valam's tongue; he knew the man, but couldn't remember his name or title. He tried to think carefully, although quickly, searching for a name to match the face, but he was puzzled and Chancellor Van'te wasn't there to whisper in his ear. What was the man referring to? Of course, he was alive. Valam tried to picture a name for the face he saw, "Mikhal," flashed into his thoughts.

"Prince Valam, we thought you dead. We thought the storm took you. Oh, thanks be to the Father!" shouted Captain Mikhal. Images spun through the captain's mind. His thoughts carried him back and swept him away.

"A storm *is* going to take us if we don't hurry!" whispered Liyan into Seth's mind.

Seth turned to face Liyan. "Yes, you are right. I sense heavy snows. An odd season, is it not?"

"More than that, I suspect," directed Liyan into Seth's mind alone.

"I am Captain Mikhal; this is Lieutenant Danyel'," said the captain as he watched Valam search for words.

"Captain Mikhal, yes, 'Lieutenant Danyel,' curious," said Prince Valam. "It is good to find you."

They rapidly went through the remainder of the introductions. As Brother Teren took the lead, the winds suddenly changed directions, bringing in a gale from the northeast. The new wind had an instant chilling effect as it touched bare skin. Evgej and Valam wrapped their cloaks tightly around them.

Evgej didn't much care for the cold; as it touched his face and hands, he cursed it. He would much rather be in the warmth of his southerly homeland. Quashan' was rarely visited by harsh cold, and even more rarely with snow. As the group turned in a northerly direction, his teeth began to chatter.

Snow descended from the sky in large flurries. Evgej was growing agitated in the saddle. He had to keep moving around to gain warmth. Evgej could see from Valam's staunch features that he wasn't reacting to the cold as much.

"Do you think he will come before the snows fade?" whispered Seth into Liyan's thoughts.

"I believe we must wait to see, but if he is a wise man, he will wait."

"Yes, as would I."

"These snows are out of place and time. They will soon trap us indoors; let us hope these men have built adequate shelters."

"We have nothing to fear; Keeper Martin and Father Jacob are smart men."

"The weather along the coast should be considerably milder than here," commented Liyan, as he squinted in the face of the heavy snowfall; a mild, tingling sensation against his face spoke of the cold without; otherwise, he did not feel it though he did think it a dark tiding.

Valam drifted back in thought. Images wandered through his

mind as life-size pictures against the white backdrop of the snow. He saw the Queen-Mother in those images, and he whispered out the name she had told him only he could call her. He was careful to use the mind controls Seth had taught him to mask his open thoughts, so his words did not drift into the others' consciousness by mistake.

Brother Teren raised a gloved hand high. Although the gesture was scarcely visible, it was seen by the rider behind him and was passed on to those behind him. Thus, the signal to halt was passed to the rear. With a dour countenance, Teren dismounted and led his mount back to Seth and Liyan. The walk was more a formality than a necessity, for he could have directed his thoughts to Seth or Liyan instead, which would have been more forceful than his spoken words.

Seth's response was just as exaggerated; he wished to continue, no matter the odds. A delay in the open plains could prove fatal; they could be snowed in indefinitely. They would continue on, even if they must travel into the night.

"Not much like home anymore, is it, Seventh?" called out Captain Mikhal to the man who rode close at his side. Danyel' waved his head negatively in response although snow wasn't that unusual a sight for him. He had spent many long winters in the northern sectors of the kingdom. It wasn't that he liked it or disliked it—mostly, he was indifferent to it.

Although Teren could no longer see his way, he could feel it. He had visited this prairie many times, as had the snows. His native sense of direction was extraordinarily strong, an important attribute of any good scout, He knew where the camp of men lay along the coast, and the Father willing, he would lead everyone to it.

A startled emotion flowed to Tsandra, who had been riding solemnly with those of her order. She steered her horse mid-group and charged without thought, issuing rapid summons for those of the Brown to follow her and prepare.

Her thoughts reached Seth and Liyan in disarray, and caused the remainder of the group to come to a sudden halt. Seth was confused, as was Liyan; they didn't understand what Tsandra had perceived. Seth sent questions to her mind, but her thoughts were scattered and unreachable.

Valam raced his mount toward Seth; his voice wavered as he shouted his questions. Tsandra's words had been sent frantically. They had been in the words of Seth's people, but he had only caught a few words. As Valam approached, it became obvious to him that Seth was also confused, yet he asked again anyway, "What is it? What did she see?"

Seth's response was that he did not know either, but she had told them to wait until she returned. So they would wait until she returned.

"Can you ask her again?" queried Valam.

"I have tried but her thoughts are unreachable."

"Unreachable?"

"She is confused."

"Confused?" asked Valam, adding when Seth didn't respond to the thought that lay heavily on his mind, "Is this what you call mild snows?"

"This is an odd storm. I assure you the coast is clear and

tranquil compared to this. The sea breezes are much more forgiving than those of the plains."

Brother Teren, also of the Brown, charged after Tsandra, screaming out, "No! Don't!" to her mind, but her thoughts were closed. He spurred his mount several times, chiding it to go faster. "What are you doing? No, don't! Leave him alone!"

Tsandra released her right leg from the stirrups, carefully securing her left. She leaned outward and downward with her arms, ready to snatch up the tiny scurrying form as it raced away. She grabbed the figure, with its legs still flailing the air as she picked it up, and tucked it close beside her, sending her followers out in all directions in search of any others.

The child muttered something Tsandra didn't understand, biting her hand immediately afterwards, causing her to release her grip. Tsandra jumped from her mount and chased the child. Her feet slipped as they hit the icy ground. As she grabbed the tiny figure again, she fell face first.

"Brother Tsandra, I implore you. He means no harm. He is my shadow," forced Teren into Tsandra's mind.

"What do you mean shadow? Why is he following us?"

"He is not following you. He is following me."

"Why?" demanded Tsandra.

"He always does. Let him go, and I'll explain."

As Tsandra released the boy, he scurried away, his short legs weaving a blur, very quickly carrying him to a distance where he felt safe. Teren pushed thoughts and images into Tsandra's mind as they hurried back to the group. Tsandra recalled her warriors and movement slowly restarted; the dark storm attained full fury during the delay and was not dealing with them kindly.

"Explain?" demanded Tsandra into Teren's mind, letting him know that it was a subtle order, which she as the first could make, and that it demanded a quick, precise response.

"He is an orphan. He has been following me for a very long time. Do not let his size fool you; he is quite capable of surviving on his own. He has endured worse storms than this, and the fact that you sensed his presence was not an accident, as you would think. He wanted you to notice him although I don't know why."

"Why haven't you found him a suitable family to dwell with?"

"He would not go. Again, you only sensed him because he wanted you to. Most often, I only know he is there by a presence at the edges of my awareness."

"Nevertheless, I caught him, didn't I, where you couldn't. I could have helped him."

"He was only playing with you."

"Playing with me?"

As Tsandra rode angrily away, Teren didn't regret her later scorn. There was no worse place she could send him to and no better. Contrary to what Tsandra thought, Teren really loved roaming the plains, even in the face of storms such as the one they now endured.

Cagan, who wouldn't have missed this trip for anything, was having second thoughts. Clumps of thick, wet snow fell upon them, sticking and forming tiny mounds and layers on clothing, equipment, and everything else it touched. He was mutely thinking that if he had remained at the capital, he could at the very least have watched the wind fill the sails of his craft while it was moored at the docks. He would have run the sails up for the occasion. But now instead of rolling waves beneath his feet, he had saddle sores.

The snowfall grew so thick that Teren thought it better to dismount and lead his horse rather than ride. There was nothing he could mistakenly lead them into along this open span. He felt closer to Mother-Earth as he walked across the thick grasses of the plains and it allowed him to maintain his sense of bearing. The animal also needed a reprieve. It was instinctively cautious about traveling under such foul conditions. Being led reassured it.

The pack animals were becoming heavily bogged down under their burdens. The group was forced to stop frequently and remove the mounds of snow from them, most especially from the protectors over the animals' eyes. The snow still had a wetness to it that made it cling to everything it touched. An animal that could not see would not move, no matter how much it was coaxed.

The thick grass they traversed still afforded them fair traction even with inches of snow piled deep onto it, but ever so rapidly the last signs of the grasses were disappearing. Teren stopped the group again and went back to counsel Liyan and Seth. Although his eyes chanced upon Tsandra, who was close-by, he did not acknowledge her presence in his conversation with the two. His suggestion was to construct a shelter here where they stood, while they still had the means and the illumination of day. Although the odd storm obscured the light, it was still better than it would be after dark.

Chapter Three

With the arrival of Nijal and Shchander, the curious company was complete. Xith, Amir, Noman, and the others would now go to the last place the dark lord would expect. They would journey straight into the heart of darkness itself to confront the darkness sweeping the land before the darkness confronted them.

Crossing the Wall of the World at night was a dangerous gamble but a gamble that was accomplished without accident or incident. The company entered the thick woodlands of the Western Territories, traveling day and night for two full days before slowing the pace. The distance did little to quell Xith's nerves. His mind was continually on edge since Vilmos left them. He had failed. He had tempted fate and lost; its sting upon him was as a thousand lashes against his innermost self. He had altered the paths, and they were now lost to him. He felt the convergence sweep in, but nothing beyond.

Yet most puzzling among his many disconcerted, disconnected thoughts was the whereabouts of Ayrian. Although intuition told him Ayrian was not dead, he could not conceive another fate for him. In his mind, Ayrian slowly ceased to exist as hope of his sudden re-appearance waned. He was greatly saddened by this because Ayrian was the last of the mighty eagle lords.

The thoroughfares they traveled, although they were the primary connection between the kingdom and the outlying cities of the territories, were wildly overgrown in many areas. Progress along them with a carriage was slow and tedious. Xith sat absent-mindedly holding the reins in much the same manner that he had chastised Nijal for previously, watching the team of horses plod along the path.

Amir rode beside Noman, honing his muscles with a series of tiny contractions and relaxations, being careful to stretch them after they became fatigued; thus, he maintained his awareness and he was not the only one in the company to feel increasing unease. He took every opportunity, although they were few, to wrest his sword from its sheath. Nijal was often his companion, willing or not, but most times willing. Shchander sometimes joined in with Nijal, making it two against one, to give Amir a challenge, but he was most comfortable watching.

Noman was also content to observe. He spent most of this waking hours reflecting on the turnings of the Path. He enjoyed the intellectual conversations he and Xith would have late in the evenings, which as of late had been of varied lengths, usually lasting well after the two should have retired to get adequate sleep for the next day's travels. Sometimes he would secretly cast the sticks, playing at the game of Destiny though he knew he should not.

Since their passage into the forest, the company had switched their practice of traveling in darkness, for the path was extremely treacherous at night even with the talented Amir leading the way. Noman put to full use the hours that would have been wasted. He sent Amir to search for any signs that they were being followed or tracked. He sent Nijal and Shchander in search of game for their food stocks, as the supplies were running short. Both searches were fruitful.

Adrina whiled away days in relative solitude within the confines of the carriage. Nijal seemed to ignore her presence since Shchander's arrival, not that she blamed him. She could see that the two were old acquaintances, and they had much catching up to do; nonetheless, she felt left out.

She picked up scattered bits of Shchander's stories of Imtal through Nijal, only enough to arouse her curiosity but not enough to quench it. She was very glad to hear that Calyin and Lord Serant were in the Great Kingdom. From time to time she would unconsciously massage the fingers of her hand, soothing away a pain that was no longer there. Nijal remained the only one who knew of the mark upon her. She told no one else and made sure Nijal didn't speak of it.

Within the cover of the forest, Xith allowed Adrina to open the central window's curtains. The view of the forest as it passed by was often beautiful, pristine, and peaceful. The smell of the evergreens with a touch of moisture from the morning's dew powerfully massaged her senses. A feeling of happiness flowed within her.

Under the thick shield of the forest, nightfall became apparent only as the last of the shadows merged and became a mass of blackness, which also signaled a halt to the day's trek.

Amir, Shchander, and Nijal worked out a suitable place for them to stop, one that offered sufficient concealment. Camp was set up in a matter of minutes; no time was wasted in obtaining food or rest. The watch shifts had long since been worked into a routine and all knew when their turn would be.

Morning arrived crisp and clear although no one within the forest's domain knew it. Amir greeted the bird's joyful salutes to the new day with one of his own, which brought immediate silence to the area around him. He had breakfast sizzling over a makeshift spit before anyone else awoke—two fat rabbits, whose juices oozed down into the hot coals, producing an aroma that permeated the camp.

Feeling a presence behind him, Amir whipped around quickly. "Morning," quietly intoned Nijal, with a smile on his lips. Amir knowingly shook his head and returned Nijal's greeting. "Good, very good. Keep up the practice, but next time don't disturb the ground you walk over."

"What? You didn't even know I was there until a moment ago."

"You broke a twig three steps back, but you are getting better," said Amir, handing Nijal a piece of meat. Amir watched Nijal eat, studying his movements before he ate. Noman and Xith soon joined them around the small fire; without a word they sat down and divided the remainder of the first rabbit between them.

"Where is Shchander?" asked Xith of Nijal.

Nijal shrugged his shoulders. He didn't know. The last time he had seen Shchander was when he had relieved him from first watch. Nijal didn't let the thought slow down his appetite. He hurriedly finished the large section of leg and grabbed another one.

As usual Adrina was the last to arrive; her face was pale and her eyes still had sleep in them. Nevertheless, she had a cheerful smile on her face as she sat down next to Nijal. She wasn't particularly hungry this morning, even though the aroma of food brought a desire to try some. She picked at a piece of meat while the others ate, and then handed the remainder to Nijal, who didn't refuse it, and just as quickly finished it.

"How many days do you estimate until Zashchita?" asked Amir, making conversation with Xith more for Nijal's benefit than his own.

"At the very least a passing."

"Two weeks is a long time."

"And Krepost?"

"I would count on an almost equal amount of time."

Nijal asked "We are going all the way to Krepost?"

"Yes, we are."

"But, I thought—"

"Nijal, don't worry. I can see it on your face."

Nijal frowned and drank from his water skin. The water tasted good although he would have preferred something else. Afterwards, he passed it to Amir, which was the polite thing to do. "But two turnings?" said Nijal, dishearteningly. "It's—"

"Such a long time," completed Noman.

"It will be gone before you realize it has passed," added Xith.

"Shchander," said Adrina, "come and eat."

"What's wrong?" she said again, waving to him to join them.

Amir readily detected something out of place. He dropped the skin of water to the ground without thought and stood drawing his blade as he did so. Nijal was next to follow him toward Shchander. Xith and Noman responded by whisking Adrina away in the opposite direction.

"I wouldn't do that if I were you," spoke Shchander.

As his words fell upon the air, men stepped out of the forest's cover. They were clad in distinctive heavy leathers and the poise of their weapons in their hands spoke of their skill. Amir slowly moved backward towards the center of the camp, not taking his eyes off Shchander, unsure whether or not Shchander supported the attackers.

Nijal moved in behind Amir and covered his back. He watched as Xith, Noman, and Adrina also moved back into the middle of the camp as their avenue of escape also closed. The four stood, watching and waiting, as the men approached, with Adrina carefully maneuvered into relative cover between them.

Chapter Four

Geoffrey's elite group paused a moment before charging into battle. Each whispered the free man's creed in their thoughts, "I am a free man, and I will die as such." The first four men moved as one, dividing the onslaught precariously between them. Quickly they defeated the attackers, splitting them into pairs that they picked apart with their four blades.

"I beg you again, Lord Serant," said Lord Fantyu. "No offense is worth a man's life, and right now we need every person here to join the fight to win our freedom. Chancellor Volnej could not be your traitor. Did you not know that King Jarom had his parents executed when they returned to Vostok?"

"I thought they lived here in Imtal until they passed."

"No, that is false," simply answered Chancellor Volnej. "King Jarom had them put to death for treason. They loved your kingdom and for it they died. Do not dishonor their memory with your words. I beg you. I am no traitor. I love this land also. I would die for it, but please do not let my end come thus. It would bring shame upon my family, and there would be none to clear my name."

Geoffrey scowled at King Jarom, who was no more than fifty

yards away, seated smugly behind the wall of his men. Words flowed from the king's mouth and a large contingent of his bodyguards moved to join the battle at the front entrance. Geoffrey and the governors reacted immediately and met them mid-way.

Sheer numbers soon overpowered them as the small force was faced with two enemy detachments coming from different directions. Geoffrey cursed and spat into the man's face in front of him, but the warrior didn't hesitate in his attack. Geoffrey offered a wry smile, and responded with a block.

Lord Serant, although puzzled, didn't have time for further consideration of the chancellor's words; his thoughts immediately returned to the fight. His thoughts had never left the front entrance to the hall; subconsciously, he had been weighing his options. He watched as the assailants poured into the chamber uninhibited; the last of Geoffrey's men had fallen. Geoffrey was alone; now was the time to act before it was too late. He had entirely given up hope of reinforcements arriving in time, if at all.

Lord Fantyu was through waiting. Before Serant could stop him, he vaulted over their blockade and charged for the door. Captain Brodst was quick to follow him, with sword in hand. He had already carefully considered the odds and had decided his own fate.

Sister Catrin shook the wavering images from her thoughts and stood. The blow to the head had done her more good than harm. She was absolved, cleansed of the dark priests' treachery. A thought stuck out in her mind, crossing from her subconscious to her conscious. She surveyed the room and gathered her bearings.

Midori's whereabouts were first priority on Sister Catrin's list as she was the first to the Mother and must be safeguarded at all cost. If Midori was safe, her next priority was Calyin. The keepers and priests offered her no concern, although she did reprimand them. "Buffoons!" she yelled.

Her thoughts paused a second more on the priests. Father Joshua—where was Father Joshua? She searched around the chamber but found no sign of him. Movement caught her eye, a struggle. She now knew where he was; unfortunately, the enemy had already taken him.

Although extremely fatigued, Geoffrey raised his blade again to defend. The shine in his eyes faded to the darkness of his weary soul. His companions fought valiantly, but they, like him, were only mortal. He did not grieve their loss. They died as they had lived, and for that he was thankful.

Lord Serant was faced with an ominous decision. He no longer expected support to come, so now he must act, but with wisdom. Princess Calyin calmly stood at his side, also carefully watching and waiting. She knew how to defend herself; and if the time came, she was sure that she would make King Jarom feel her wrath.

Lord Fantyu sidestepped the first attacker to charge; as he did so, he pushed the man directly into Captain Brodst's waiting blade. The warrior fell to his knees clutching the blade as he went down. Captain Brodst retracted his blade and stepped over the body to Lord Fantyu's side.

Catrin's mind worked quickly and similarly to Midori's. She held no hope of reaching Father Joshua. Although he would have been the most suitable, she turned to the other priests. She did not take back her words of moments ago in any way; she only did what had to be done.

Midori had identical intentions running through her mind as she rapidly assessed each in turn. The priest with the strongest will was her choice. She thought he would be a good choice, even more than Father Joshua. Now she had only to reach him. Sister-Catrin had chosen the same priest to link with, but Midori was the first to reach him, and he willingly conceded to the link of the Mother and the Father; together they would unite the two wills and unleash their powers upon King Jarom's forces. They would make him pay.

Chancellor Van'te and Chancellor Volnej, although up in years, held fast to their positions beside Lord Serant and Princess Calyin as they all sought to escape. They held their blades, a short sword the captain had discarded, and a long dagger from Lord Fantyu as they followed Lord Fantyu and the captain, lagging only a short space behind them. They stood proudly, defiantly, in the separation between Lord Serant and Lord Fantyu, waiting and ready.

A defensive position only served a purpose as long as it held the hope of adding to one's resistance. Lord Serant no longer saw such a purpose for the spot they were in. He saw only an end if they remained—a sure, absolute one. His mind was clear although it was alive with scattered observations. Movement was the only alternative he saw that remained for them.

Midori felt a whirlwind of power collide in her center as her will joined with that of the priest beside her. She prepared mentally for the ripping force of the Mother and Father to flow through them as they became one. Although she had never felt it before, she knew it must come. She waited, holding her breath in anticipation; it did not come. Shocked, she backed away from the priest, her eyes wide with disillusionment.

Midori, in disbelief, formed the union again. She quickly completed the link, only momentarily pausing before she joined. She felt the force of wills connect within her, as she had before, but the warmth did not flow to her. She saw no images in her mind; the link quickly fell away, and she knew unequivocally at that moment that the Father and Mother had abandoned them.

"Now!" screamed Father Joshua, with all his strength, to his compatriots as he was being subdued. He reached out for the will of the Father, which he could not find. He attempted to scream a warning to his brethren, but a gloved hand sealed his mouth. The priests of the Father descended into the swarm of invaders, pushing them back momentarily.

Lord Serant seized the opportunity. He grabbed Calyin by the hand and clutched it tightly, indicating that she should follow him closely, and that he loved her. Carefully, he scrutinized the field before him. He made a direct line to the right of the hall, straight for King Jarom, and, he hoped, freedom.

Lord Fantyu was quick to note the direction Serant was taking. He and the captain held a line safeguarding Lord Serant and Calyin's passage, slowly moving alongside them, while the two chancellors prepared to block to the right although the only thing ahead in the direction they moved was a large group of King Jarom's body guards, who stood steadfast at their positions.

As they made a headlong charge towards the group, it became obvious that King Jarom had not anticipated such a maneuver, as his attentions were directed to the priests' demise. He was taking great pleasure, as one by one they fell before his men. His voice boomed throughout the hall with his hideous, raucous laughter. The others seated beside him did not share in his joyous mood. King Peter and King Alexas sat with faces rigid, afraid to look about the hall but not ashamed of their deeds either. They were quite grateful that Andrew rested with the Father, for now they had no one's revenge to fear. King Charles held his head low in shame; he had had no choice but to concede to King Jarom's wishes.

King Jarom's guards were slow to move and react, as their king had ordered them not to move and they greatly feared his scorn. They did not move to engage until Lord Serant and the others were fully upon them.

Father Joshua managed to raise his voice about the hall one more time before he was belted across the head, and his world faded to black before his eyes. "Ywentir, never forget!" His words were enough to incite fury into the keepers' hearts, and enough to motivate their disheartened spirits, and the final spell dissolved.

Lord Serant said a hurried prayer to the Father as he saw the keepers stir to action. Lord Serant told Calyin to follow the two chancellors wherever they took her and to stay with them at all cost. His voice fell on the last word as he dove, arms and sword stretched wide, onto a group of guardsmen, knocking three of them down with him.

Lord Fantyu masterfully pummeled with the hilt of his sword while blocking another blow with his blade, the hilt catching his would-be assailant directly in the face.

As he blocked the second, he brought his knee up into the man's groin, followed by an elbow to the back of the head. Captain Brodst cleaned up to the right, while Lord Fantyu attacked again to the left, his overbearing power with a sword readily apparent as he sent blows of metal against metal, bringing the edge of his sword always to flesh.

King Jarom's verbal abuse against his men was enough to stir them into frenzied, thoughtless attacks. Serant was quick to his feet. He didn't waste any time, as he covered the two chancellors and Calyin's retreat. He could see the door was within their reach as he turned back toward King Jarom. Only four men separated him from revenge, which his honor demanded that he have.

Lord Fantyu felt a sudden cold feeling that sent chills running up his back. Numbness swept over him. He bit his cheek; his sword did not falter as he followed through, bringing another of the enemies down before him. He felt the blade withdraw from his back, and winced, but he continued to fight.

"Don't be a fool!" yelled Captain Brodst to Lord Serant, "Get out of here now!" He pushed Lord Serant out of the way and engaged the two who stood before him. As he turned to sweep through with his sword, he saw the blade withdraw from Lord Fantyu, but he could not move to help him. Anger flowed through him and into his hands, as he hammered down with all his might on the foe before him.

Lord Fantyu moved in close beside Captain Brodst. His

energy visibly slowed as blood dripped from his mouth. "Go! I'll cover you!"

"I will go nowhere! I'm here to cover you, remember," spoke Captain Brodst as he blocked.

"Like you covered my backside!" said Lord Fantyu, sounding harsh, but not meaning it. "Go before it's too late!"

"If I go, you're coming with me," said Captain Brodst, as he blocked again.

"We'll stand and fight together, my friend."

"Yes," said the captain as he watched Lord Serant hack down the last man who stood between him and the door, safely making his exit.

"Are you ready?" asked Lord Fantyu, as he watched a group of warriors break through the disarray in the center of the chamber. He elbowed the captain to gain his attention in that direction momentarily. Geoffrey of Solntse yet lived. He was buried amidst a mass of bodies. Only the glimmer of his full-handed sword raised high caught Lord Fantyu's eye.

Lord Fantyu was slow parrying, and a blow glanced across his shoulder, slicing through his mail, but not wounding him. Captain Brodst paused, and instead of attacking, he opted to defend quickly both right and left, taking the brunt of two attacks momentarily to give his partner a reprieve. "Have you said your prayers?" asked Captain Brodst, indicating they should push forward to where Geoffrey stood.

"Yes, I am ready to go, but not until I take a few more of them with me," grunted Lord Fantyu, as he struggled to maintain his balance.

"If we go, it will be together!" added Midori, as she and Catrin finally managed a short retreat to the spot where the two stood. "Through there—" she further added, indicating the door to the antechamber. "Yes, but first we will help out our friend," said Lord Fantyu. "We cannot abandon one with such skill and bravado."

Chapter Five

"Brother Teren, I believe we must continue on. We cannot afford to stop now. We will push through the night if necessary."

"Yes, I back Liyan also. As you have told us, you promised Keeper Martin and Father Jacob we would arrive within the week. They need these supplies we bring."

"Brother Seth, Brother Liyan, I hear your wisdom, but you do not know the nights on the plains. It will be unbearable."

"We will endure; we must endure. I believe you can get us safely to the coast. I trust in you."

"As do I," added Seth.

Brother Teren, devout in his commitment, pulled the hood of his cloak up tight around his face and walked back into the face of the storm. The wind blasting south only added to the tumultuous flurries surging from the skies overhead. He noticed a conscious twinge of power against his will and cast a feeling of impatience back at Tsandra.

At a lethargic pace, the party began moving again. Teren was very careful to insure that the entire group was behind them as they did so. As he reached his thoughts back to the last section, he was sure all was in order, and he increased the pace ever so slightly.

Seth urged his mount to move onward though the beast would have preferred to remain still. He whispered to Liyan and then moved back to where Valam and Evgej rode. Seth voiced concerns to Valam over their previous debate. Evgej was quick to add that he was also concerned.

"This storm, what will it be like when it is at its full fury?" asked Evgej.

"Its power comes and goes. It is a natural cycle."

"This is not natural," directed Liyan to the three.

"What do you mean?" asked Valam.

"Brother Seth and I have been discussing this storm and its origins. I believe it is not natural, that it is an omen. A dark omen."

"Have you spoken with Brother Teren about this?"

"We have considered it, but will wait till a better time."

Evgej offered a scowl, to which Valam quickly appended, "I think we should have that discussion now. Brother Teren knows these plains."

Liyan nodded to Seth. Seth rode off in search of Teren. Shortly afterward, Liyan joined the brothers of the Brown. Valam could see the elder riding alongside Tsandra. Tsandra cast glum stares in Valam's direction as the night moved quickly in about them, carrying with it more cursed cold.

The snowflakes became crystalline as all the moisture in them solidified. Contrary to what Seth had hoped, the snow did not stop, nor did it slow; it maintained its barrage on them ever so efficiently.

The bite of the cold, especially in places that they could not adequately cover, grew beyond numbness to pain. Valam removed the gloves from his hands and touched the warmth to his face. A burning sensation swelled through his cheeks and nose. No matter how tightly he wrapped his hooded cloak about him, it did not shield his face.

Valam and Evgej were at a disadvantage as the darkness fell about them. They did not have the gift of Seth's kind to communicate amongst themselves with thought. He doubted his tongue would move if it were necessary; or perhaps, he thought, it would freeze solid mid-sentence if he attempted to speak.

Captain Mikhal and Lieutenant Danyel' followed closely behind Valam and Evgej. Cagan made up the fifth of their tiny group. In front of and behind the five stretched a long caravan of horses and riders although they were the only such grouping amongst the entire party. They rode with a length of rope between them to mark their distances as visibility faded to obscurity. The others had no need for any such bonding. They had their link.

Liyan searched the sky with his eyes, looking for patches of scattered heavenly light, but he saw only blackness. He cast a sour feeling to Seth's mind, to which Seth responded with an equally glum expression. After hours of riding through the darkness, Liyan felt as if they had only moved inches; to him it was if the winds held them at bay and for each step they moved forward it pushed them back an equal measure.

A feeling of despair surged amongst them and even though they would not admit its presence, it was there. They were as weary as the animals they rode upon, especially those heavy with packs. Liyan's propensity for thought was muddled by his exhaustion, another feeling which was pervasive; luckily, his other faculties were still mostly intact. Common sense told him they must stop now, and Liyan answered its call.

"Brother Teren!" he called out with his mind. "We must rest, the animals as well as ourselves."

"If we pause, we will not be able to begin again," answered Teren.

"As you said earlier, this I know."

"If it is your will, then it is so."

"It is."

"Then so be it," responded Teren in thought, while he reached out and touched the minds of those who followed him as one. "My brothers, we will wait out the storm here."

"Can we survive the night here?" asked Liyan, of only Teren's mind.

"If it is the Mother's will."

Tsandra approached the foremost group. "Why do we stop now?" she demanded of Liyan; the words were a spontaneous reaction to Teren's thought. She did not even consider the possibility that it was Liyan's idea that they stop until she reached out with her words to his center. As she did so, she bit back further comment.

"How can we endure this cold?" asked Seth, as he dismounted. Scattered sparks of light lit the sky as torches were raised on the extreme ends of the party. The lights were drawn together as the group formed a closely packed circle.

"The answer, Brother Seth, is beneath your feet."

"The snow. How brilliant!" answered Seth as he touched Teren's mind and Teren's thoughts. "What of the animals?"

"With luck, they will survive also."

Seth returned confused thoughts; Teren had obviously been in this situation before. Teren led the way and the others followed his example. He raised two mounds of snow around him and formed them into walls. Teren explained as he moved through the steps. He positioned the junction of the two walls into the wind, raising it upward to shield him from the chilling effects of the wind.

Cold, tired bodies moved cold, tired hands in a fevered attempt to raise a shelter from the storm. The first thing they did was to release the burdens from their animals and then they followed Teren's example. Teren showed them how to form the walls together, connecting in a series of staggered angles.

The work stirred warmth into their muscles. Seth paused a moment and slumped down beside Teren and Liyan. Valam and Evgej also took a moment's reprieve and joined them. Evgej closed his eyes as he sat down; the warmth returning to his body felt so good. "Do not let the lull of warmth blind your thoughts, Brother Evgej," whispered Teren, "the warmth will carry you off into the winds of the night."

"Say that again," said Evgej, drowsily.

Teren touched the palm of his hand to Evgej's brow. He held it there only a second before he removed it.

"Valam, Seth, remove the gloves from his hands. Liyan, pull off his other boot," thought Teren into their minds quickly, as he removed Evgej's right boot. "Quickly remove his cloak. Seth, remove your gloves as well. Follow my example." Teren washed Evgej's foot in the snow, massaging the foot with his hands. "Seth, can you feel the will within him?"

"Are you mad?" screamed Valam, "The snow will kill him!"

"Valam, please just listen to me, or else Evgej will die."

"Yes, but it is shallow."

The urgency of Teren's message within Valam's thoughts was all the proof he needed of Teren's sincerity. From then on, he did exactly what Teren told him to do. "Evgej, can you feel this?" asked Teren as he pinched Evgej's foot.

"Yes," responded Evgej.

"Can you feel this?" asked Teren again.

"Yes."

Teren looked to the others; he had not touched Evgej's foot a second time. "Keep massaging his hands in the snow," Teren told the others while he talked to Evgej. "Can you feel the movement of your fingers?"

"Yes."

Teren told them to stop, and asked the question again.

"No."

"Good, good!" responded Teren. Teren continued to work frantically over Evgej, directing the other three as he went. "This is exactly what I feared. We must be astute during this night, or none of us will reach the morning." Teren carefully chose words to remind all present of the effects of the cold against their limbs and their lives. Forcefully, he reminded them to remember above all else to keep moving. "Do not let your bodies slow. Guard your will. Maintain close watch over your mount. Do not let it wander away, but make sure it also stays mobile. Be wary. If one bolts, all the animals will bolt."

"Will Evgej be all right?" asked Valam. His mind bristled with thoughts, none of which were pleasant. He wondered how Captain Mikhal and Lieutenant Danyel' fared, as they also were not used to severe cold weather. He blamed himself for Evgej's condition; common sense should have told him to ensure Evgej was wary.

"Yes, I believe he will be fine, but we must keep him warm," responded Teren while he directed into Evgej's mind another question.

"Ouch!" yelled Evgej, "That hurt!"

"Good! Keep moving your toes."

The amount of wood they had for burning only amounted to a scattered stockpile of torches, which would provide little heat even if they threw every last one into a pile and burned them. Besides, they needed to save the torches and a dwindling stack of wood used for cooking. It wasn't much, since most of their food stocks were dried, but at best they could warm their ale over it, which is what they decided to do. They were given the opportunity to get warm liquid into their bellies before they settled in to endure the remainder of the long night.

Fortunately, the cold had not deeply touched many others. Valam surmised from what he saw that Seth's people had a much greater tolerance for the cold. Valam dreaded the many sleepless hours that lay ahead. As he saw Captain Mikhal and Lieutenant Danyel' move from the long line huddled around the dwindling fire, he motioned for them to join him.

He was sitting alone. Seth and Liyan had helped Evgej to the fire. The three were still there, sitting around it. He could see from the expression on Evgej's face that life was returning to his veins. Captain Mikhal and the lieutenant followed Valam's lead and sat upon their packs, to avoid sitting on the cold earth.

The walls of snow shielded them well from the chilling effects of the wind, but the storm's rage still found its way to them. "How do you think Keeper Martin and Father Jacob fare?" asked Valam of the captain as more of a conversation opener than anything else although he was interested in hearing more about the two.

"They are tough men. I am sure they are fine," replied Mikhal.

"Do you know much of these plains?"

"Yes, we have been very thorough in our scouting."

"Then you were on a scouting expedition from the camp when we met you?"

"Well—"

"Yes," responded Danyel'.

"How many days had you been away from the encampment?"

The captain paused, and then Danyel' answered the question, "I had been gone from the camp three days when I met Brother Teren. He had seen something that piqued his interest and asked our group to ride along. Unfortunately, Keeper Martin sent Captain Mikhal in search of my group when we did not return to camp on time. They met up with us just hours before we met your group."

"Then, Captain Mikhal, you probably know best how affairs are at the camp. Are spirits good? How goes the training?"

"Training goes well."

"Have you been able to carry on Seth's training?"

"Yes, you would be surprised at the enthusiasm. After the initial confusion, or should I say rather bluntly, disdain, a certain fascination caught most everyone."

Valam nodded his head in approval. Silence fell between them, and Captain Mikhal muddled over thoughts in his mind. He considered telling Valam of Keeper Martin's plan to return to the Great Kingdom if supplies did not come. He didn't know how Valam would take news like that. He just hoped the keeper and Father Jacob would hold out an extra week as they had planned although tomorrow would mark the seventh day of his absence.

"Tell me more of the lands in the vicinity," requested Valam, ever shifting his thoughts to concerns for the future. "Seth has told me a little, but I want to hear it from a viewpoint I can relate to. Have you seen signs of the enemy?"

The captain and the lieutenant took turns depicting all the details they could recall about the countryside they had explored. Valam was very careful to note each detail they gave him; his mind fed on them. The picture he created in his mind helped him feel more at home here, even under these inhospitable conditions.

As the last embers of the fire fell, Seth, Liyan, and Evgej, with help from the other two, moved back to join Valam. Full feeling had returned to Evgej's joints and limbs. He felt much better although he did still feel rather foolish. He had felt fine until Teren had started prodding him.

Evgej smiled a half-smile, and offered Valam the remainder of the warm ale in his skin, which Valam only accepted after Evgej assured him that it was the third skin that had been forced upon him, and he could not drink any more for some time. As Valam sipped the warm drink and its warmth spread through him, he was reminded all the more of the cold that was present all about him. Only a few more hours to go, he told himself.

The beat of Valam's heart increased as the first, tiny vestiges of light appeared on the horizon. In that instant, Valam thought to himself that he had never seen a more beautiful sight. But as he watched, the tip of the sun broke the horizon, and he realized an even greater sense of elation. For the first time in what seemed an eternity, he saw the blue of the sky.

"Evgej, isn't that magnificent!" exclaimed Valam. "Evgej?" shouted Valam when no response returned. "Evgej? Seth?"

Valam jumped to his feet, "Evgej? Seth?" he yelled wildly. He strained his eyes to focus in the coming light. He squinted. Captain Mikhal and Danyel' stood a short distance away. Liyan sat next to him, his concentration lost while he wrung his hands, trying to keep them warm, but Evgej and Seth were gone.

Valam moved down the line of forms in the immediate vicinity, first to the right, and then to the left. He shouted their names again, stirring Liyan from his thoughts. "Liyan, where are Seth and Evgej?" Liyan shrugged his shoulders; it was evident he was also puzzled. He had not noticed their absence either.

With the coming of morning and the life-giving essence of

light, the camp quickly sprang into a bustling hub of activity. The snow stopped. It was a miracle. There was much to be done, but the first order of business was to rescue the supplies from beneath the white blanket where they were buried. Teren was quick to order an accounting of all, including animals and equipment.

Tsandra watched him with contempt in her eyes, but in her heart different feelings were stirring. She almost felt sorry for him. Such a desolate place to endure one's life. What a waste, she thought to herself. The brightness of the sun seemed to return feeling to her cold, tired body immediately. She checked over her own mount and her personal effects. The animal had survived the cold better than she had.

As the minutes swept by, the darkness was swallowed by the brightness of the new day. Valam's eyes continually adjusted to the changing light. His search for Evgej and Seth had taken him along their makeshift shelter, peering into every corner he chanced upon. He finally found them at the far end of the wall. Seth stood upon a large mound of snow, with Evgej beside him.

"Evgej, Seth!" shouted Valam.

Evgej was quick to note Valam's mood and he replied, "We're fine. Idle minds and hands are a waste, that's all." He stooped down and patted the mound of snow beneath their feet, which must have been a full ten feet high. Valam felt foolish for not noticing them, for as he walked towards them they were totally in the open. If he had been looking up or even straight ahead instead of down, he would have spotted them easily.

Valam clambered up to the top of the mound. As he reached

the summit, he shielded his eyes from the glare of the white cover all around them. Valam released a gasp of amazement as he looked about, "Wow!"

Teren's voice called out to Liyan, Seth, and Tsandra's minds. "Five dead, and eight beasts gone." He spoke simply; nothing more needed to be said. Teren, as did the other three, held their heads for a moment of silent prayer, and then moved on to other matters. They counted their good fortune; the dark storm could have claimed them all.

Teren counted his good fortune twice. The snows had ceased, the morning sky was clear and bright, and with luck they would reach the coast by late afternoon if his estimate were correct. But first they must excavate the camp. The wind had piled the snow several feet deep in many areas, even with their protective walls. It would be some time before they would be ready to travel again.

Chapter Six

"Shchander, how could you?" shouted Nijal, "I counted you a friend."

"As do I," said Shchander.

"But why this treachery?"

"It was not I," said Shchander.

"Who then?"

"Think about it," said Shchander, subtly indicating those around him.

The distance separating the two forces diminished as the others closed in. Amir swept forward in a crazed fervor. As he sought to gain a clear opening, he met and matched the blades of the attackers many times. Angrily, hand over hand, he swung his blade back and forth circling his body from left to right, back to front, with finesse and ease.

Although his blade covered a full 360 degrees around his body in the blinking of an eye, his assailants did not hesitate to engage him. As a group, four men circled him warily while the remainder of their compatriots moved inward. Their attacks were swift, accurately timed, and precise. Simultaneously, four blades reached for him, only to be just as swiftly denied their target.

Xith drank in the energies around him; he cursed himself for not fully gathering a reserve. He had let his guard down; he would not let it happen again. Energy seeking to come to life touched his fingertips but was not yet alive with power.

Surprise was tough for Noman to handle. His response, however, was in no way slowed. He quickly tossed up a shield about the inner circle, which was effectively sealing them from attack by any projectile.

Nijal had been decisively cut off from guarding Amir's rear by a clever ruse. An additional group composed of a complement of four, guarded his every movement. His prowess with a sword did not match Amir's, but he held his own and kept them at bay.

Amir raised his blade high and thrust, quickly followed by a block left and right. He ducked to avoid the attack from his rear, whipping around to knock the blow upward. Followed immediately a second time into the opening in the attacker's defense, he recoiled as metal striking metal resounded.

The blow should not have been blocked; how could it have been? He gathered his senses close in his mind, and then cleared his thought to a new way of thinking, adapting always as he had learned from the plentiful lessons Noman had given him. He was impressed by his new opponent's prowess.

Xith poised with energy raging within him. The magic was clear and clean at his center. He needed only to give it form. For an instant before he did so, his thoughts slipped to Vilmos. "Oh, the waste," he whispered, "such waste."

Nijal sucked air heavily as perspiration dripped down his face. It was all he could do to defend. He didn't have time to attempt even a simple jab; his mind was fully focused on survival. His sword arm swung through block after block, switching from a clockwise rotation to a counterclockwise rotation as the attacking force necessitated.

Nijal's blade clashed heavily against one of his opponent's glaives and the sting knocked him back. A series of attacks left and right knocked his blade from his hand. Suddenly, Nijal felt as if his heart had stopped beating.

Noman raised his hand to stop Xith from releasing his magic. "Wait," he told Xith. Noman raised his voice loftily to Shchander, "Point well taken. I accept."

"How did you know?"

"You are clever but not overly so. Your desire gave you away."

Dismayed, Nijal accepted his sword as it was returned graciously to his hand. He was beset with confusion. He couldn't comprehend what Shchander had done. Warily, he maintained his distance from the warriors who stood immediately around him, staring at him with coy expressions on their faces.

Amir sheathed his weapon without another thought and without hesitation. "You fight well," he complimented the swordsmen around him, "as one." Amir moved to a position beside Noman, patiently waiting, but yet wary. Wary not because he doubted Noman's abilities, but because it was in his nature, and intuition told him to act thus. He made sure Adrina was close at hand.

"These men are well-trained, as I have told you," explained Shchander.

"I know, my friend, but the point is that we need to move quickly and maintain a low profile."

"If you will not take us with you, then we will be forced to take you with us," said Shchander, raising his sword to join his compatriots, as such was his conviction and his promise. They raised their weapons as well, moving quickly to re-engage.

Noman noted the determination set into Shchander's features and responded in kind, "My mind is set. I can see now that we must travel together." He paused, and then as Shchander smiled and lowered his weapon, Noman exclaimed, "Take them!"

Adrenaline pumped through Amir's veins as he withdrew his sword from its sheath. He looked forward to another test against such worthy fighters. Having learned from the previous encounter, he noted in his mind their movements. He would not make a similar error again, but he also noted in his mind that these were not true enemies, and he would not be severe with his weapon's edge.

Nijal was hesitant to react; these were men of the same blood as him. They were no enemy. He could not raise a weapon against an ally; it was against his code. The dilemma beset his mind, but it did not delay him from defending as he felt the swish of a blade nearly rake the side of his head.

"Shchander, give faith, my friend. Noman knows what is best; this I believe with all my heart."

"The test of swords never hurt a man, especially not a free man. Provide me this jest."

"You always were a man of words," grunted Nijal as he strained under the weight of a blow. He was wild and arcing in his defense, wielding his blade like an apprentice.

Amir studied the four within his mind, contemplating the tensions in their muscles, trying to reach into their minds and feel when they would attack. Shifts in the air about him, smells potently clinging close about him, sounds of agitated hands tightly clenching, or the expirations of breaths heavy into the air, all spoke of their movements in Amir's mind. He circled and moved, blocked or guarded, independent of their individual movements. Now he was fixed on the four as if they were one because now within his mind they were.

Noman reassuringly put a hand on Xith's shoulder; he was more intrigued now that he knew it was only a test between them. A test that he was sure would be anything but easy. He was captivated by the complexity of the fighters' movements. It had been a very long time since he had seen men with such promise, and although he was confident that Amir would win the challenge, he looked forward to watching.

Instinctively Amir edged closer towards Nijal, seeking to use Nijal as a cover for his backside. A similar notion passed through Nijal's thoughts, and he slowly led his assailants in Amir's direction. Amir followed through with a clean series of blows, while Nijal absorbed the necessary blocks.

As Shchander joined the strife, it was nine against two. Under the circumstance, even Amir's skills were being worn away although he was enjoying every moment of the challenge. He had not been so thoroughly tested since they had left Solstice Mountain. He recalled the last hours there with disgust.

"Give up, my friend," said Shchander, "do you not recognize

the training?" Shchander maneuvered to split the two up again and divide their defenses once more. For now, the two could hold them at bay while they came in at them, taking each attack as a wave. It was clear: the swordsmen were also taking care not to cause serious injury.

Nijal knew what Shchander was referring to, but he answered slyly anyway, "No, I never had the time to learn from him." Nijal sighed in relief after the words left his mouth, as the edge of a sword sliced the air just short of his neck. One of the swordsmen winked at him, which angered him. Amir quickly returned the favor, and the swordsman lost his air of haughtiness.

"That is a shame; you have his prowess, you could have had his knowledge also," chastened Shchander as his block clubbed Nijal's blade heavily. Two other swordsmen followed suit immediately with a thrust, while a third attempted to knock the blade from Nijal's hands.

"I chose a different path; this you know," said Nijal as he winced from the pain of the stinging in his hands. Amir poured his strength into his blade and drove back his attackers again.

"Yes, but you know oft times he is right."

"In no case does that give you absolution. We will fight."

"Then so be it," said Shchander as he drove in with his blade, blocking up, while two other swordsmen attacked Nijal. Amir whirled around to face Shchander. At the same time, Nijal displaced the sword from Shchander's hand. The sting of it was evident on Shchander's face as it grew red with surprise and rage. "Don't be so gregarious when you fight, my friend. You lose your concentration."

Shchander very graciously bowed to the victor, picked up his sword by the hilt, and said, "We are finished here." Shchander motioned to his compatriots to lower their weapons and follow his retreat, which they did without contest. Shchander sheathed his sword and walked away without further delay.

"For that, there will be no need. You have doubly proven your worth," said Noman, raising his voice loftily. "Come. We must make haste. It is time we departed this place."

A broad smile lit Shchander's face, and the faces of his fellows. Nijal moved to embrace Shchander, "You are correct, though. You have learned well in my short absence."

Shchander nodded his head in response. He was too tired to speak any more now. He understood that Nijal implied his skill of leadership as opposed to his skill of arms. One of the swordsmen motioned to catch Shchander's attention, and he waved back, signaling it was permissible to retrieve their mounts and supplies.

"Come," said Nijal, indicating Shchander should follow him. Nijal went to see to their own animals. The two then assisted Amir as he reconnected the team to the carriage; Adrina was already seated inside, ready to go. She smiled at Shchander, as he passed by, and for the first time, she accepted his presence and approved of it.

As they departed, Xith wasn't the only one scouring the heavens for a presence just on the edge of his consciousness. He was certain that his use of magic had given their position away to someone or something unseen. He could see that Noman felt it as well, as did the mighty titan, Amir.

Chapter Seven

Dark shadows suddenly fell over the hall; scattered thoughts brought hesitant glances to vaulted windows set high along the east and western walls. The windows were designed to fill the chamber with light from dawn to dusk. It could not already be nightfall, thought Captain Brodst. "Had the battle lasted that long?" he wondered.

"Geoffrey. We must reach Geoffrey first!" yelled the captain.

The four surged forward, straight into the onslaught of their assailants. Captain Brodst wasn't surprised at all as he watched Midori hold her own in battle. She had, after all, learned from the same master he had although matched daggers offered no reach compared to a full-handed sword.

Lord Fantyu bit back the pain in his side, and vaulted into the enemy. At least now the invaders were dividing. King Jarom had ordered all available men to chase down and capture Lord Serant and Princess Calyin. The scorn rang evident in his words as his voice boomed over the top of the cacophony of battle.

Geoffrey was also grateful for the slight reprieve, but the advantage was still on the side of the enemy. Words muddled in his mind as his frenzied thoughts slowed. He still did not think he would survive, nor did he hope to, but now he would surely take more of the vile wretches with him.

As the mass of bodies thinned out, Geoffrey saw Lord Fantyu and the good captain for the first time. "Flee!" he shouted to them, "Flee!" although now with both exits fairly secured, he knew the opportunity was gone. Captain Brodst lowered his head for a moment; they were going nowhere.

Midori reached out with her mind, straining to find the will of the Mother. Her consciousness still spun with disbelief at the absence; how could the Mother abandon them in their time of need? As dark shadows lighted over the hall a second time, she hesitated, but slowly her attention was drawn westward, up the raised rows and beyond to the vaulted windows. The sun was indeed setting.

Wearily, Lord Fantyu raised his sword; the clash sent his body reeling. His knees wanted to collapse under his weight, but he strained to hold on. A second blade reached for him; Fantyu moved to block, but he was too slow to recover. He moved to dodge, but he was struck full in the mid-section. Although the gleam of victory was in his opponents' eyes, Lord Fantyu did not lower his gaze.

Captain Brodst's eyes were wide with rage as his blade crushed downward; the two forces collided. Brodst's blow was clearly stronger; he drove through, severing the opposing weapon unmercifully from the other man's hands. The contempt was evident upon his face as he plunged the tip of his sword deep. He watched as the man fell, careful to move around him as he toppled, making his way to his next foe.

Catrin grimaced as she dodged an attack. She was quick to send her daggers home into the man's gut, thrusting upward to reach his heart. Her first blade found its mark as did the second. She laughed as his blood ran bright down her hands to the floor. She held no pity for his soul; she would make them pay for their evil deeds.

Geoffrey sidestepped a blow while he parried a second. He fought to gain back the offensive, but he couldn't get any blows past the two who blocked his every move. A third moved to his side. Geoffrey stopped just short of tossing an elbow into the man's chest. "Captain Brodst, you old son of a wood troll!" he yelled.

Lord Fantyu wavered as his thrust was knocked harmlessly back at him. He perceived a presence to his left and right, Midori and Catrin, but he knew they were too late. He was beyond their help. His countenance held firm, almost regal, as he raised his sword to counter one last time. A surge of adrenaline swept over him as he launched himself full onto the enemy before him.

Two blades sank deep, piercing cleanly through, reaching outward, as Lord Fantyu fell upon the other. A trickle of blood pouring from his mouth spoke of his demise, but the smile held to his lips as he looked into the eyes of the one who lay beneath him. His aim had been true. He breathed in his last breath.

A tear fell from Midori, rolling crystalline down her cheek. She knew without a doubt that Lord Fantyu had passed. The remorse on her face was quickly banished, as she immediately moved to re-engage. She had paused only an instant to say a prayer to the Mother and to the Father. She hoped they would still hear her words even if their will did not walk through her.

Both Geoffrey's and the captain's minds were jolted with a burst of speed and anxiety. They had seen Lord Fantyu fall; similar thoughts moved through their minds. The military mind within them carefully tallied the odds: now they only numbered four.

Midori raised her voice to a pitched, venomous screech, the effects of which were not lost on those around her. Even the most stalwart of figures cringed as the sound pierced their ears. Steadfast, Midori turned the instant's hesitation into an advantage as she lunged. Daggers level, she descended upon her prey, evil justice in her eyes.

King Jarom stood and turned to face Midori. "Kill her!" he shouted to his henchmen, "Kill her now!" Jarom feared those of the Mother as much as he feared the dark priests, both of which had their uses at the proper time. But now was not the proper time, and he had no use for their sort. He would have his fun with the priests they had captured.

He chuckled as he watched his men turn with new vigor. The attack was taking longer than he had planned, but he liked its progression thus far. In a short while, the kingdom, all its subjects and domains, would be his. He would make sure there were no heirs, apparent or otherwise; even now his servants sought out all those of royal lineage.

"Finish this. I grow weary!" he barked at his remaining bodyguards save two, which he motioned should stay. Afterwards he also sent his captain to urge those following Lord Serant and Princess Calyin. King Jarom smiled and turned to the other kings.

All save one were calm. "Do not fear, King Charles, I hold no grudges."

King Jarom smiled as he walked over and patted King Charles on the back. "All is forgotten," said Jarom as he lifted his jeweled stiletto from its sheath. King Jarom fiddled with the blade in his hand while he stood behind King Charles. He watched as Charles thumped his fingers against the tabletop. Charles lurched in his seat as Jarom placed his hands back onto Charles' shoulder. Charles sighed in relief and his heartbeat returned to normal.

Catrin spun around and clipped the arm of her opponent, her blade visibly raking into his leathered armor. The man's blade fell to the ground as the tendons in his hand were severed. A gasp of pain came from his mouth. Catrin was quick to follow through with a second slice to the jugular, ending the dispute.

Geoffrey signaled a series of short, defensive retreats so the four could better handle the additional onslaught, which, when coupled with those streaming in from the hall, was utterly overwhelming. It took concerted effort just to make the retreat effective. His eyes sought out a place in the room, which offered little maneuvering; his only hopes were to draw out their demise.

Captain Brodst began kicking chairs at those who covered their retreat, carefully making sure to maintain his balance as he dropped back over the body-strewn floor. As he had a few seconds to think, he reflected that he did not regret his life; he had lived fully. He hoped with all his heart that the lord and the princess had found escape.

Catrin staggered backwards as she slipped across the floor. One of her daggers fell from her grasp and bumped across the floor. She was quick to recover and turned in wild retreat, striving to catch up to the others. As she turned, she caught a blade mid-shoulder, which stunned her to her knees. Her hand stretched out, but no one could help her now; she was beyond them.

Midori stopped cold, and whipped the blade in her hand around to feel the tip between her fingers. She scoffed as she withdrew her hand, and flung it at the warrior who stood so gallant retracting his blade from his victim. The blade caught him clean, low on his neck, just above his armored collar.

The three withdrew all the way to the farthest reaches of the room, fighting their way up the raised platforms, up the rows of benches, to where they did not know. All options suddenly came to a halt as they reached the far wall; there was no place left to go. Geoffrey grimaced as he realized that he had backed into the wall.

"Till the end!" he shouted, as he threw his blade aside. He reached his hands out wide, ready to embrace all those that came near. He hurled himself downward, putting all his strength into the vault, and adding all his weight to the force. As he slammed head first into the closest two, they sent a shock wave rippling down to the last bench, knocking them down along with all in their path.

The waning light suddenly gave way as the last rays of light disappeared with the sun beyond the horizon. The room fell to darkness and shadows, as the glare from the windows above faded with the light. A loud ruckus broke to a roar, immediately following.

"Till the end!" shouted Geoffrey, as he lifted himself up off the floor, bringing his fists into contact with anything available.

He flailed wildly about himself, hitting anything and everything around him. A brawl broke out around him, and as none could see in the darkness, no one knew who was hitting whom.

"Get them! Kill them!" shouted Jarom, infuriated. He moved close to the two guards beside him, quickly groping his way back to a chair, and a feeling of relative safety. His curses grew above the noise of the fighting, inciting anger into the minds of those who listened. His voice raised, ranting and raving louder, demanding torches be brought in at once, threatening all who failed him with immediate punishment.

Minutes later, the first torches were carried in from the adjacent halls. King Charles smirked at the collapse of Jarom's bravado, which even in the shadows was garish. King Jarom was quick to plant the apex of his stiletto dead center between Charles' eyes, sending him reeling backwards, flailing his arms, dead as he dropped.

Geoffrey had edged his way out of the fight, under the cover of darkness, moving skillfully on his hands and knees. As the torchlight brought sight to those around him, he was caught. He poised his eyes pleading up to the heavens, raising his hands, and shrugging his shoulders.

"Not this day!" he yelled to Jarom as he leaped to his feet and up to the captain and Midori, who had been standing at the ready, waiting in the darkness for whatever came their way. Geoffrey clasped his hands together, "Up you go!" he indicated to Midori.

"Where?"

"Hurry, put your foot into my hands. Don't ask questions. Just do it."

The puzzled look on Captain Brodst's face vanished as realization hit him. His countenance changed to an expression that said, "Are you kidding?" But he was quick to assist Midori up to the sill. Afterwards, he stood motionless for a heartbeat. His eyes moved to those that were only seconds away from them. Captain Brodst interlaced his fingers and said, "Go!"

Geoffrey shrugged his shoulders, "No. Set your blade there, and be quick about it!" Geoffrey had snapped it at the captain like an order, to which Captain Brodst was quick to respond, not because he wanted to, but on impulse.

"But where do we go from there?" asked Captain Brodst, as Geoffrey boosted him up. As Captain Brodst moved upward, clenching his fingers against the wall, pulling himself also upward, his face reflected his confusion. His face also reflected his gratitude.

"The choice is yours!" shouted Geoffrey in response, as he grasped the captain's sword.

Chapter Eight

The city of Zashchita lay only days ahead of them at the far edge of the forest; in retrospect, it seemed to be cut out of the forest. A few leagues away from its lookouts, the forest began anew. Noman knew this, as he knew the sun would rise in the morning. Vast ranges of forests cut across the face of the territories—too much—thought Noman. He looked forward to the time when they would reach the sea and cool, coastal breezes.

The humidity in the forest seeped into his skin and his soul. He breathed in the moisture from the air around him. Three days of rain filtering through the trees had set all in gloomy moods except Adrina. It wasn't because she rode inside the carriage, which was dry, but because the rain brought fond memories. She liked the slight feeling of sadness the raindrops gave her; in an odd sort of way, the sadness actually lifted her spirits.

Adrina thought about the words Noman spoke to her when they stopped. She dwelled upon them. A pain in her stomach caused her to wince, and she leaned her head out the carriage. The fresh air against her face made her feel better, but the queasiness still did not go away. After she got rid of her lunch, her stomach settled down, at least temporarily. Her hands swept down to the mark upon her belly. "Tnavres," she said quietly to herself, "Tell your master, I will never do what he asks."

The carriage jolted to a sudden halt, and Noman jumped down from its seat, as did Xith. In front of them, Amir and Nijal also dismounted. Storms had knocked down a group of trees that blocked the road before them. Noman quickly calculated the options; the forest was too thickly overgrown with underbrush to move around the trees, especially for the coach. The choice remaining was the obvious one, move the trees, which would not be an easy task.

Amir yelled to Shchander and his men to move up from the rear and assist, but by the time he yelled, they were already coming. Hours of toil and sweat later, their combined might moved the first tree a few feet. Amir looked to Noman in frustration but would not give up.

He scratched his head and told the others to put their backs into it this time. On his mark they began again, grunting and groaning as the eleven of them strained beneath the tree's weight, which was going nowhere. Nijal stopped and stripped down his gear, as if it would help, as did the others. "Again," signaled Amir.

Sweat pouring down his face, but with no lessening of determination, Amir called them to a halt minutes later. As he slumped down, spent, the others also rested. After a brief respite, he stood and slapped his hands together, spit into them, and rubbed them together again.

Anger was evident on his face as he motioned for them to give it another try. The others followed without hesitation or complaint, putting every last ounce of their strength into one last attempt. Success lighted Amir's face as they moved the tree from the ground, albeit only inches; slowly they walked it back. They had moved it about a foot when it became clear it was stuck and wasn't going to budge anymore.

Xith and Noman called them to a stop. They decided that they would try magic to levitate the carriage across, as opposed to wasting the entire day trying to move the trees. "Unhook the team," called out Noman. Adrina stepped out of the wagon to watch the spectacle.

Xith looked to Noman. Both had hoped to avoid the use of magic or its forms for as long as possible as much as possible. It might give away their position, a thing they did not want to happen, especially if the enemy did not know where they were. He slowly began building energy within himself, taking it in from the energies around him. Odd, he thought to himself, the energy wasn't as strong here as he would have expected.

Amir looked amused as he watched Xith struggle to gather the power within him. He watched and thought about the problem and came up with a new solution. He signaled to Nijal and pointed to the carriage. Shchander hesitated, but his men joined in without him. Amir and Nijal picked up the rear of the wagon while the other eight lifted the midsection and the front. They squatted and lifted in unison, surprised at how light it seemed compared to the tree.

With a few groans and grunts, they made it over the barrier of trees and placed the coach on the opposite side. Noman was quick to laugh at the simple resolution of the dilemma, but also quick to stop Xith from drawing in any more energy. Xith stopped, looked, and took a second look before he realized what had occurred, but he was also quick to grin in relief that the obstacle had been overcome.

In a short while, and after a short rest, they were moving along the trail again; thoughts of the rain, the humidity, and Zashchita, were for the moment forgotten. Shchander and Nijal broke into light conversation about their home city of Solntse, and the grudge between them also lifted. Nijal insisted that Shchander retain the title of captain. Nijal was fairly settled on the fact that he was not ready to return to Solntse any time soon to regain his office; and if Nijal had his way, Shchander would return to Solntse once they safely reached Krepost' on the edge of Statter's Bay.

Noman was perplexed. Concern played heavily on his face as they rode on, bringing a furrow to his brow. It was something Xith had said to him just as they had departed that had sparked the consternation. His fears caused him to lose track of everything around him as he turned inward. There was a presence in the farthest reaches of his thoughts that he could not grasp.

A shadow passed over the sky above unnoticed. Xith rode in the coachman's seat beside Noman, still a little miffed at the proceedings. Xith fiddled nervously with his fingers, the touch of them against each other was wrong.

A breeze, albeit slight, began to stir, moving through the trees with a whisper. Subtly, the temperature began to change, and the air around them became cooler as the humidity dissipated. Noman and Xith were not the only ones fidgety; the oddities around them played on Amir's senses, made more perceptive by his blindness.

Adrina drew in a quiet breath; the sudden coolness brought on drowsiness. She watched the trees pass with their leaves of green, brown, and gold. Her eyes grew heavier and her breathing slowed, and then she drifted off to a light slumber. Her thoughts were mostly pleasant as she shifted to a deeper, peaceful sleep.

The trail became dense and twisted; large overgrown patches were in rich abundance. Thick shadows formed beneath the trees and as they moved deeper into the shadows the light of day slowly faded. The trees around them spoke of ancient times; their forms grew as thick and tangled as the path.

The harbinger of night fell quickly upon them although it was far from dusk. They found themselves huddling closer together. Even Adrina, who was sleeping soundly now, suddenly felt solitude, a great separation between her and the world around her. Spontaneous reactions brought many hands to the hilts of weapons held yet in their scabbards.

They waited with bated breath, fingers playing restlessly against hardened metal, minds filled with images of looming horrors. Gloom sank into their souls, creating specters in the trees. Without realizing it, they slowed to a lethargic, careful pace.

Minutes became hours as the seconds ticked past, a heart beat at a time, a breath at a time. Every sound caught the ears of the listeners—a trodden stick, a moving branch, the breeze rustling through the trees. Nervous eyes darted from side to side in anticipation.

Shchander motioned for his companions to split up and ride alongside the carriage, four to a side, while he went to the front.

He cast his eyes towards Noman and Xith, shrugging his shoulders. He wanted to ask, "What is it? What is wrong?" for surely they must know the answer, he thought, yet his mind told him not to break the silence.

Xith returned Shchander's gesture—he did not know. Something weighed heavily upon him although he could not touch it. Absent-mindedly, he rubbed his palms with his thumbs. The minute spark of energy created as he did so trickled across his thumbnails.

Ahead, the growth around them grew sparse, but the darkness did not dissipate. It loomed around them, clinging to their souls. A clear disjoining lay ahead and as they passed it, the shadows seemed to lift. Then as suddenly as they had come, the dark clouds overhead scattered.

"Help me! Somebody, please help me!" screamed Adrina. Her body was fixed with convulsions, "Help me!" she whimpered.

The coach came to a sudden halt, and Adrina was jolted backwards into the padded seats. She lay there trembling, afraid to move. "Make them go away!" she yelled. "Make them go away!"

Two large figures unfurled the doors to the carriages and leaped inside. They stared blankly at one another. The coach contained no one save them and Adrina. "Princess, there is nothing here. You are alone."

"No, they are here!" she cried, her eyes pleading with them to listen to her.

"Adrina, are you unwell?" yelled a familiar voice.

"Xith, please send them away! Make them leave!"

"Please," said Xith, "leave her alone." Xith indicated that the others should leave and he took Adrina's hand and led her outside. "What is it, dear?" he asked sympathetically.

"Please send them away. Make them go!"

"Them?" asked Xith, pointing to the two who had just returned to their mounts.

"No, not them. They are there," said Adrina, pointing to the inside of the carriage.

Xith peered into the interior of the coach, "There is no one there. It is empty."

"No," cried Adrina bursting into tears. "They came for me. They want me to go with them."

Xith was confused and worried. He glanced at Noman, subtly asking, "Is there something there?" Noman stepped down from the buckboard, and inspected the carriage. Afterwards, he shook his head negatively. He saw nothing. "You must have been dreaming, my dear. Everything is fine now, I assure you."

"No, it is not," replied Adrina. "They have come for me because I won't do what he asks."

The way she said it sent chills down Xith's spine. He looked to Noman again for assistance, then to Amir and finally Nijal. Nijal took Adrina's hand and returned with her to the coach. As Nijal stepped into its confines, Adrina froze cold, her face fixed in a mask. "No," she repeated. She would not step within.

"Adrina, I assure you there is nothing here," said Nijal, sitting. Adrina held firm. Nijal stood and took her hand, pulling her inside. Adrina became hysterical. She started screaming and shouting frantically, tears welling up in her eyes and streaming down her cheeks. "Please, no," she said pitifully.

Nijal held her hand warmly, caressing it, soothing her, slowly coaxing her to step in. "There, there," he whispered to her as she leaned her head against him. One small step at a time, he drew her into the carriage, and they started anew although all were a little shaken. They would be very glad to have this section of the forest far behind them.

The remainder of the day proceeded smoothly. They set up camp just as dusk came on. Xith was still puzzling over what Adrina had said. He tried to help her by talking about what she had dreamt, but Adrina would not talk about it. Fear was still evident in her eyes, and she did not want to be left alone this evening. That was clear.

Nijal took the cushioned bench across from Adrina as they lay down to retire for the evening. He watched her as she lay there for hours with her eyes wide open. "What is it?" he asked softly.

"Nijal, can we sleep outside tonight?"

Nijal thought about it for a time, and as he did so, Adrina said, "I will not get dirty. I will be fine on the ground. I do not need special comforts." Nijal agreed, but he would not allow her to simply lie on the ground. He woke Shchander and his men, and the ten of them gathered a nest of pine needles for Adrina to rest upon. The light seemed to return to Adrina's eyes as she lay down to sleep.

✳ ✳ ✳

Father Jacob paced nervously in his command tent. He was alone. Captain Mikhal had left in search of the seventh, and

Keeper Martin was gone, to where he wasn't sure. If he were not a holy man, his curses would have been foul. He did not like the dilemma he was faced with. How could they leave, but how could he justify not leaving? He had given his promise to King Jarom and to Prince Valam, but he had also given new promises to Keeper Martin.

"Why did I let him leave?" rang his voice loudly about the empty command tent. The page outside the tent quickly entered and stared at him. Father Jacob waved him away. "Be gone!" he yelled. As the page retreated from the tent, Father Jacob caught a glimpse of the sky outside; it was as foul as his mood, which sent him deeper into his rage.

He walked over to the table and stared blankly at the half-filled charts strewn across its surface. He cast them aside and unrolled several more from a trunk near the table. His heart fell heavily as he examined the coast of the kingdom. The next chart contained hastily written remarks that Jacob couldn't decipher—winds, currents, times, and cycles with blank spaces and question marks, which Jacob assumed were estimates, or better yet, guesses.

Fatigue suddenly overwhelmed him, as it had often of late. He slumped into a chair, sitting motionless until his breath returned. He again threw the charts aside, cursing Keeper Martin as he did so; immediately, he unrolled a piece of parchment and began hurriedly scribbling.

Hours later, as he finished the scroll, he placed it with the other scrolls of his account, careful to secure them with lock and key in a small chest, which he placed back into the larger trunk.

The page hesitated before entering, clearing his throat to ensure that it was okay to come in.

The page set Jacob's lunch on the table, meager as it was. Rations were extremely low even for one of Jacob's stature. Jacob had insisted on equal rations for everyone including himself. With his face set in a mask, Jacob ate and for a time cleared his thoughts of all matters, even those of a pressing nature. As he finished, the page came back and took the plate, exiting without uttering a word.

The food sat thick and warm in his belly. Jacob sat still for quite some time, staring emptily at the wall of the tent. Anxiety and exhaustion coupled with internal turmoil brought him to the verge of collapse yet again. He had not slept in days, as was evident by the hollow shells of his eyes.

"Was it all for nothing?" he asked himself as his world faded to blackness. The camp was at the brink of depleting its last food stores; the little they had would only last a few more days at the most, and that only if they continued the strict rationing. They had only enough wood to maintain meager fires for cooking and little else. Water was the only thing they had in abundance.

Images played through his mind. He recalled distinctly the day they departed Imtal, the sojourn to Quashan', the trek across the dark waters, reaching the Eastern Reaches, but most clear in his mind were the emotions in Keeper Martin's face as he triggered the ancient device and disappeared. Jacob could not tell if it was surprise or shock or horror; nonetheless, Martin was gone now, and he, Jacob, was alone.

Chapter Nine

As Lord Serant broke into the courtyard, clutching Calyin's hand followed by the venerable chancellors, his mouth fell agape. In astonishment he watched as the sun was swallowed by darkness, piece by piece. Frenzied thoughts ran through his mind. Thoughts of escape suddenly became secondary.

Calyin jolted to a halt as she stumbled into her lord. "What is it?" she asked, before she registered what was evident. She raised a hand to her mouth. A flicker of movement caught her eye on the far side of the courtyard as she peered heavenward.

Chancellor Van'te sank to his knees because of the agonizing pain in his side but also from awe. Chancellor Volnej quickly followed. "Father?" he cried, the word springing from his lips before he could cut it short.

The air turned cooler and a light breeze moved in as the shadows swept toward them. On the far side of the courtyard, a figure ran toward them, exhaustion clearly showing on his face. Lord Serant paused, also regarding the figure moving toward them. From a distance, Lord Serant couldn't tell positively who the figure was. He did not know whether to flee or stand and fight.

As the figure approached, Lord Serant became certain that it was Swordmaster Timmer, as he had thought. The swordmaster dragged his right leg and draped his sword over his shoulder as he moved toward them, surprise and relief on his face.

"My lord, you are safe!" he hailed. "Thanks be to the Father."

"Swordmaster Timmer, what has happened? Where did they all come from?"

"I do not know, my lord, but we shall make them pay for the treachery; this I promise."

"Where are the garrison troops? The palace guards? Pyetr?"

"A few of the guards were with me, as you know. We have fought our way from the armory. I am afraid it was the first to be taken; only a few of my good men survive. We escaped the ambush. They are pushing into the inner castle as we speak. We did not know where you were, my lord."

"The garrison troops, are they not in the city?"

The swordmaster shrugged his shoulders; he had dispatched men to inform them, but they had not returned although he thought that the garrison troops had surely seen the siege. "Where were they?" he thought to himself. "Come, we mustn't delay here. It is not safe," spoke Timmer, eager to move from the vulnerable position of the garden area.

"Where is Pyetr?" demanded Lord Serant.

"I do not know; come my lord, princess," said Timmer with concern in his voice. He cast his eyes often to the sky as they retreated.

"Where is there safety?" asked Lord Serant. "Is the whole of the palace under attack?"

"I am afraid it is. There are so many. Damn it, where are the reinforcements!" Timmer cursed. "Are there others yet in the great hall?"

"I pray so," said Serant in hushed, reverent tones.

"We will reach them, don't worry. It will be just a matter of time as reinforcements arrive."

"How many men do we have now?" asked Lord Serant.

"Scattered pockets, I am afraid. We were taken by surprise. Vile treachery, I tell you. We had no warning."

"In all?"

"Several detachments, four squads in all, managed to escape with me; they are within the palace now."

"Is that all?"

"I am afraid it is. They descended upon us in a swarm from all directions. It is a miracle that any of us escaped at all."

Lord Serant hung his head; his thoughts were grim. He stopped just before they reentered the palace, looking at the shadows play upon the sun. It is an unnatural thing, he thought. It can only be an omen, an omen of ill tidings. He raised a defiant fist at the sun, and shook it angrily. He swore under his breath; he would make all who were responsible pay.

Movement through the halls proceeded slowly and cautiously; constantly they changed directions, moving away from the sounds of fighting. Slowly, they were being led around in a circle, being pushed back out into the courtyards. They were too small a group to venture an encounter. They could escape only if they avoided engagement.

As they entered a section of the old palace, ascending many

floors and backtracking through the old private hallways and corridors, Calyin took the lead since she knew this area the best. Although she had not wandered these paths for many years, she still knew every detail from the time she had spent in them during her childhood. She brought them to a place where they could look out at the front courtyards, which lay behind the palace gates, and see the square just opposite the wall.

The sights from both views were ominous. A large contingent of black-clad warriors poured from the square through the gates. Within the courtyard was turmoil, a sea of bodies moving and clashing, mostly waves of black with tiny sections bearing the green and gold of the Great Kingdom. Lord Serant staggered back from the window, confused and dismayed. Fatigue swept through him, a sudden weariness that came from his soul.

Carefully circumnavigating the open passageways, Calyin brought them back to the old sections of the palace and to windows that looked down into the courtyards of the armory and a section of the garden. Although they noted no movement and no signs of the enemy intruders, the scene was nevertheless startling. Fields of bodies lay scattered across the grounds as if they had fallen from the sky.

Lord Serant closed his eyes. He considered plans for escape, which seemed the only alternative left to them. The odds were definitely not in their favor. He wondered about the fate of those they had left behind in the hall. He thought them perhaps lucky. They did not have to look at what he saw now.

Suddenly, Chancellor Van'te clutched Serant's hand. "How did my brother die?" he asked. The weariness of his voice spoke volumes.

Lord Serant said with great sincerity, "He died with honor, honorable sir."

"Good," weakly responded the chancellor a glint of pride in his eyes. "Good-bye, my friends."

Van'te collapsed, still holding Lord Serant's hand as he fell. Lord Serant remorsefully closed the old man's eyes. The last expression fixed on the chancellor's face was happiness, and Serant felt that the chancellor had indeed found peace.

"Look!" cried Calyin, as she stared out the window, not in disrespect for the chancellor, but because her eyes had welled up with emotion. "There!" she said pointing. Although the sky was shrouded in darkness, a beam of light bathed a section of the courtyard. In the midst of the light sat the white gazebo of the garden. They took this as a message and hurried to that spot.

Oddly, when they came upon the open walkways, none thought to look for danger before entering, for in such beauty they knew there could be only safety. Shadows lingered in the air above them. As they drew nearer, the ray of light diffused and became many patches of light, one of which was on a window high above, though none of them was aware of this.

As the day turned into night, all the warmth was drawn from the air by restless breezes. The small company stood upon the dais of the gazebo and gazed upon a raven-hued sun. Its light was no more. They did not look at it, knowing that they might be blinded.

"Please forgive my transgressions this day, Father," crossed each of their lips more than once in the moments that followed;

but still they waited, standing still upon the platform, for the thing that had brought them here had not yet arrived.

Shards of glass struck the stone of the palace and plunged downward. Raised eyes could make out the figures stepping onto the ledge even in the darkness. Those that remained constant saw the others emerge from secret places within the courtyard as the force that drew them gathered all.

Timmer raised his sword in his trembling hands, facing those that approached. Lord Serant was quick to catch movement out of his periphery vision. He stepped in front of Calyin, raising his sword, placing himself between those that approached and his beloved.

"Your weapons will do you no good. We have long since passed and they will do you no harm," spoke a voice, crisp and clear, with melodic hints of song in the words. Hesitant, Serant, Timmer, and the chancellor lowered their blades. Calyin's stance had not changed at all. She had noted the arrival but was not afraid.

"Who are you?" demanded Lord Serant.

"Listen close, and listen well," bade the voice again, wavering in rises and falls as it spoke. "We have only a short time before we must leave. Do not fear us, but do heed us."

"But—" interrupted Serant.

"Foolish one, be still. Wait and I will tell. With three you are free and you are seven. Find it destroyed by the first, and you will endure the second."

"Yes," said another, as Lord Serant made it clear that he wished to speak.

"What is it we seek?"

"He that is learned, and he that is wise, and he that you despise."

"Find the place of old. There then will your answers lie," chimed another.

Lord Serant attempted to speak again, and another began to speak. Her words flowed cool and soothing, gentle to their ears, "When you find him, he will know."

"How do we escape?"

"You have only to try."

"Where is it we must go?"

"Through the rain and towards the sleet, beneath the toil and the heat, downward, inward, outward, upward, under your feet."

A minute tracing of light fell from the sky. The figures raised their hands to the questioning eyes and crept back to the places they had emerged from. As the figures receded, so did the other creatures that had been drawn. Vile were their faces as the glee and hopes of tasty morsels faded.

"Wait, do not go!" yelled Lord Serant. "But what of Imtal? I must stay."

A faint voice echoed back to him. It was hard to hear the words, and he strained to decipher them. It almost sounded as if the words had been, "Go you shall," yet it also could have been, "It will fall." As he thought about it, he decided perhaps it was both.

Under the light of a dawning day, two figures moved across the rooftop, followed by a third. It was the reflection of light from steel that brought their attention to the small group in the gazebo. Calyin started as she studied the pair closer. A sputtering of the wind caught strands of long, dark hair, and blew them as they did her own. "Midori!" she exclaimed.

Timmer squinted and stared. His eyes were old and untrue, but judging from proportions in the changing light, one was a woman or a very thin man. Chancellor Volnej was sure as he looked closer, as was Lord Serant—the long, flowing black hair was a distinctive trait of all three sisters.

The fastest way to reach them was to move straight through the central towers, which is what they sought to do. Lord Serant took the lead and Timmer took the rear, hobbling along but still able to move surprisingly quickly. The stairs were more difficult for him, but with Volnej's assistance he was able to make the climb at a fair pace.

"The roof, how do we get to it?" he demanded of Calyin, without thinking of the effects of the bluntness of his words. His anxiety was at its peak, and the aggressiveness of his soul had taken over his actions. Calyin glared at him and walked around him, taking him to a window that offered a ledge.

"Take care," she whispered to him while kissing his cheek as he moved out of the window onto the ledge.

"Stay with her!" he barked back at the other two, who had been unsure of what to do.

Without giving it another thought, he turned to look for the others to mark their progress, nearly falling from the ledge as he did so. Calyin shuddered as she watched him inch along the edge, slowly disappearing. Lord Serant cursed the slickness of his boots and his own shortsightedness as he stumbled a second time, clinging to the masonry above only by his fingertips.

Out of the corner of his eye, he watched the progress of the third as well as the first two. It was difficult at best to make out the forms without stopping to turn to look at them, but he did not have time for that. He was sure that one was Midori and the other the captain. The closest window they could escape into lay midway between him and them, but the other was now only a few feet away from them. He thought about shouting a warning to them but decided not to do so lest they be discovered.

He waited until they had passed the corner. Perhaps then the time would be right. He checked the sword sheathed at his side, both out of habit and to insure that it was near. If only they could reach the window, he thought, then he would surely have a chance at stopping their pursuer.

Midori was the first to see the approaching form in front of her along the wall. Her hand faltered along the wall, causing her to lose her balance and slip. Only the captain's agile hands were able to catch her, nearly pulling himself from the wall as he did so, but his grip held firm.

Lord Serant gasped, and called out, "Watch out! Behind you!" The sound of his voice brought alarm to Captain Brodst's ears at first because he had not realized anyone else was on the ledge with them, but as he registered the sounds, he placed the voice. The timing of Lord Serant's alarm couldn't have been more wrong, for as the captain's attention was distracted, his fingers slipped.

He pushed Midori against the wall as he fell. His eyes went wide with fear and desperation. Captain Brodst scrambled, clawing at the very air about him, attempting to grasp anything that lay near. Pain numbed his bloodied fingers as they tore into the lower ledge where his feet had been.

"Be gone!" cursed Lord Serant. "Death will be too good for you if you harm him!" Lord Serant shimmied as fast as he could, mustering all the strength and dexterity he could manage. "I warn you do not move!"

Lord Serant's heart dropped to the bottom of his feet as the figure approached Captain Brodst, leaning down to pry his fingers from the ledge. "Midori, get in the window! Hurry!" called out Lord Serant. He paused long enough to draw a thin blade. He reached back, taking careful aim, preparing to release only when he was confident he was direct on target.

For the first time as the figure leaned over to offer the captain aid, Lord Serant saw the man's face. "Geoffrey? Can it be?" he asked himself. Abashed, he dropped the blade. It fell tumbling, clinking against the stone as it plummeted downward.

"Oh, thanks be to the Father," he cried out, as he thought, with three you are free, and you are seven. Utterly amazed at the revelation, he did not move for a long time. He stood frozen in deep thought, contemplating the many things that had seemed foolish to him moments before. The words, he thought, the words were not gibberish; they held meaning.

The captain and his rescuer had already gone through the window and were calling back to him before Lord Serant regained his senses. Filled with emotion, he grabbed them both in a mighty bear hug and immediately afterward swept Midori off her feat. A heavy burden had been lifted from his heart.

He told them where the others waited, and they made a quick exit. A silence fell. Speech was not necessary as long as they had survived.

Calyin was filled with emotion as she and Midori met. The two sisters felt closer to each other now than they had since childhood. The exchange of emotions between them in these moments would bind them for life.

Fearing discovery, especially if anyone else had glimpsed their movements, they departed. Captain Brodst knew the obscure corridors of the palace as well as the two sisters, so he took charge. He conducted them to the far end of the upper level, coming upon a set of stairs that led to the rear armory.

As they descended the stairs reaching the final landing, Captain Brodst met a pair of cold, bitter eyes. The sword guarded in the hands spoke volumes to him as his life passed before his eyes. A single, monosyllabic word escaped his lips before he drew his sword. "Why?" he asked.

"I wanted to see the light leave your eyes as your world collapsed beneath you as it did from my mother's."

"But I loved your mother with all my heart. It was not my fault."

"Oh, yes it was."

"You are no son of mine."

"Then am I the bastard you fostered with the regal whore?"

"Step aside, for I could not kill you. To wallow in your charity would suffice my honor."

"You will not find escape!" cried Pyetr as his sword fell from his grasp.

The captain looked clear into Pyetr's eyes as he slumped, pained, against the wall. He lowered his eyes with shame and stepped passed him. The others behind him said nothing as they, too, passed by. Lord Serant stayed the call for blood that desired to move his trembling hand. He also understood that sometimes to live was a greater transgression than offering oneself to die. Pyetr would take his own life and pay his atonement in full.

Their retreat was short, for none knew where to go or what to do next; and as they reached a place they thought secure, at least for the moment, they began to argue and tempers flared. Calyin and Midori soon separated themselves from the other three, who ceaselessly debated without gaining ground.

"I will go nowhere; Imtal is where I belong," said Captain Brodst obstinately.

"You must! Can you not see that the city has fallen?"

"Lord Serant, something has clouded your wisdom. You cannot believe the words you are saying. The capital is far from doomed; if we fight, we will most assuredly win it back."

"Think, man! You know what has occurred. Do not let your pity blind your vision. We cannot wait here much longer."

"Lord Serant is correct," interrupted Geoffrey. "If we hope to escape, it must be soon. We do not have time to waste. I say we go to Solntse and return to Imtal with the garrison troops. My men cannot have deserted, nor can the garrison troops here from Imtal be very far off. They must have been sent somewhere. By my hand I will have the traitors swinging if I discover any— begging your pardon, of course, Captain Brodst. I shouldn't have said that."

"It was due me and I take no offense, but I could no more kill my own flesh and blood than I could kill a loyal servant. I believe time repays all those who are untrue. All the same, I still think we should stay here."

Calyin and Midori were conversing separately from the others. Calyin was telling Midori in great detail the words of their mystic visitors and Midori was listening with very earnest ears; something in the message caught her interest. Midori held her thoughts until Calyin had told her everything she could recall.

"I know the place," announced Midori as Calyin finished. She stopped and then mumbled something Calyin thought was, "Towards the rain. Interesting." Midori stepped between Lord Serant and Geoffrey to move towards the window. She had been listening also to the words of the three men behind her as she had been following Calyin's story. "Solntse, it is," she said, agreeing with Geoffrey.

Captain Brodst was quick to cut Midori off from further speech as he turned back to Geoffrey asking, "What are you saying?"

"Yes, what are you saying?" asked Lord Serant.

Geoffrey didn't respond; he liked the additional vote for Solntse and wasn't going to say anything either to add to or detract from Midori's statement. "Toward the rain," repeated Midori, and she pointed to the eastern sky, which was dark with heavy rains in the distance. "East is where we need to go. Solntse is east, so we will hopefully appease two of you. But what do you say, Captain Brodst?"

"Do you honestly wish to leave? I cannot believe what I am

hearing from you, Midori."

"My good captain," returned Midori, "I believe what I have heard, and I think if we put our heads together we will find that the riddles are quite easily solved."

"She is right," said Calyin.

"We do waste time here, do we not?"

"Yes, but we must first find a way out of the city."

"We have only to try."

Chapter Ten

Valam, Seth, and Teren moved through the deserted camp wondering where everyone had gone. They searched through tent after tent only to find them empty, abandoned. Glumly they proceeded towards the center of the camp, reaching the command tent last.

Valam dismounted, he hoped, for the last time. As he cast the flap widely aside, it caught the wind and pushed back at him. He clipped it with his arm and entered. The tent was empty like all the others, save for a chest in the center.

He dropped to his knees and opened the chest. Its only content was a plainly bound book, a ledger of sorts, guessed Valam. Rapidly, he scanned the first two pages, gathering from this that it was a journal, Father Jacob's journal. He quickly turned through the pages of the chronicle, skipping to the last page.

Confused, he turned back several pages and started reading again. "What did he mean, 'Martin is gone and I am alone'," thought Valam. He read forward again, closing the book as his eyes fell upon the last word. Valam dropped the book on the ground, running from the tent, "Captain Mikhal, where are the ships? Are they near?"

"Just south," he replied distantly, "about a half hour's ride along the coa—" The captain stopped mid-sentence. "They didn't?"

"I am not sure. Come!" Valam shouted as he mounted, spurring his horse frantically, "Let's find out!"

Valam instructed most to wait in the camp until he and the captain returned, but a handful followed the two as they raced southward. Valam shouted to the wind, "No, Jacob, don't leave!" to which Seth returned, "I don't believe even my thoughts could reach him, my friend."

"Is he already gone then?"

"I don't know. We are too distant. As we draw closer, I will try."

Tsandra followed close behind Teren and the others; she was not going to be left behind. Captain Mikhal spurred his horse to the lead, as he knew the way best. Ahead of them lay low-lying hills, mostly a series of short inclines and declines that occurred only along the coast.

The shore they rode along reached out into the sea via an outcropping of rocky crags. As they rode, the shoreline changed, weaving back and forth from rocky outcroppings to straight-line earthen bluffs, which the water was slowly eroding away. In the distance, as the captain promised, lay a sandy-beached inlet, where the ships should be waiting.

Seth reached out with his thoughts, trying to reach a consciousness that could understand his words. At first he just called out with a name, and then a simple message, "Wait!"

hoping the strength of his will could breach the distance. He retreated his will when he perceived that nothing lay ahead of them. He hoped it was just that he could not reach whoever was out there yet.

Teren veered right suddenly as if struck, coming to an abrupt halt. He thought he felt a tug of a consciousness upon his mind, but the voice he heard could not be here; it did not belong to the plains. Teren turned back to the path and began again, casting off the thoughts.

Seth and Tsandra also felt the voice touch their farseeing minds, but only Seth returned the call. Nothing returned to him as he reached out, and he rode on in silence. Tsandra whispered to his mind that perhaps they had all been mistaken, which Seth accepted.

The snows had barely touched the coastal areas, but a thin layer of it still clung to the frosted ground, and not far away it lay in deep mounds. They rode as those possessed, knowing their travel-weary animals wished to rest. Other thoughts pervaded the riders' minds; they were also weary and did not have time to waste.

As they approached the inlet, which was still a good clip away, the tip of a mast seemed to protrude above the line where the shore appeared to join the sea. Seth reached out again with his mind and perceived a presence. "Wait! Do not go!" he yelled outward.

Valam released a sigh of hope. He hoped what he had read in the last pages of the book were not true. He did not understand everything he had read, but he hoped the closing was false. In his mind he pictured the last page, and slowly his eyes led him to the last paragraph, which he re-read again in his mind. "By the time you read this, we will have returned to the kingdom, our home; do not hold ill feelings toward us for we waited as long as we could endure, and this the last I write in honor of Prince Valam, who, among others, gave his life for your lands. Say a prayer for him so that he may rest in peace."

Father Jacob had always been long-winded, thought Valam as he returned from his reverie. As was Keeper Martin, he added a moment later. His thoughts soared as the white of a sail grew before his eyes. Indeed, it was only a small tip, but it was a sail, he was sure.

As they drew nearer to the curve of the coast which led into the inlet, it became readily apparent that many ships floated in the small harbor, not just one. In their thoughts, they sang for joy; it was a beautiful sight. Seth called out again, in thought, and told them who they were, and why they had come. He registered great surprise in many of the minds he touched, and one almost collapsed with shock upon hearing the sound of his voice.

Those on the flagship sent out a message to the other ships, which had also heard Seth's message, and were already commencing the orders to lower their sails and weigh anchors. A longboat launched from the lead and made for shore and was soon followed by a second one from a different ship.

"Brother Liyan, no, you must leave," directed a voice into Liyan's mind alone.

"We cannot."

"They must not see him."

"It is too late."

As the group was ferried out to the flagship, a single rider faded into the distance. Valam sighed as the waves sent a calm sweeping through him. He thought perhaps Cagan should have come with them; he would have enjoyed the ride immensely. Later, as an afterthought, a shudder ran down his spine as he watched in thought as a boat sank into dark churning waters.

The trek from shore to the ship was short, and soon the oarsmen were maneuvering the longboat gracefully along the port side of the waiting vessel. Valam accepted the outstretched hand as he stepped up to the deck, taking in with a single glance the whole of the ship from aft to stern as he did so. He was greeted with surprise and disbelief, and certain awe intermingled with relief and thanks.

"By the Father!" exclaimed Father Jacob. "We had given up hope of supplies ever reaching us and behold what they return with!"

Father Jacob hesitated as he reached out for Valam, a hint of doubt touching his lips. "I am real!" replied Valam. "Believe it!"

"I do, but for so long I have thought you had passed."

"No such luck, I am afraid."

Valam's reply brought a smile to the father's deeply worried face. "You must tell me everything! Don't forget anything! But wait—wait until later," said Jacob as Valam began to speak. "First things first. The supplies?"

"Yes, Father Jacob, the supplies are here although for a time we thought you weren't."

"I am sorry. I lost my faith, but it was only momentary," said

Father Jacob. As he talked with Valam, the embedded lines in his face seemed to lighten and the weariness of his soul began to disappear. So much had been heavy on his mind lately. It was a great relief, a breath of fresh air, to see Valam's face flourishing with color, with life.

"How long will it take to unload these boats and return to camp?"

"Not very long at all," said Father Jacob, winking, "we have only men and horses aboard and few supplies. You will be surprised how fast they unload when the word is spread that Prince Valam, or should I say King Valam, has returned."

Father Jacob bit back any further words. His tongue had slipped; he had said too much. The fatigue had not so easily left him as he had thought; his mind was still not as sharp as it ought to be. Father Jacob hoped that perhaps Valam had not understood his words, but his looks gave everything away to Valam. Any sense of happiness left Valam's face as he realized the import of Father Jacob's words.

"When? How? How long have you known?" pleaded Valam, retaining his composure, but stuttering over his words.

"I do not know for sure," began Father Jacob, choosing his words very tactfully, "perhaps—no, not perhaps. Prince Valam, I am very sure. Come, we should withdraw to my cabin for a time."

Father Jacob was quick to note who was close at hand and could also have overheard their conversation. He was glad to note only Captain Mikhal, to whom he offered a glum smile as a greeting, and Brother Seth, whom he indicated should follow. They were the only ones close enough to have overheard his conversation. The others behind them, none of whom Father Jacob knew, were told politely to wait. Tsandra was the only one who was offended.

"Why did you not return to the kingdom at once!" demanded Valam.

Father Jacob looked hurt and did not reply. He was attempting to gather his wits before he opened his mouth and said anything further. Valam mistook the silence as another opening to lash out, which he did harshly.

Father Jacob quietly spoke the words that he would have preferred never to repeat. Quickly and precisely he brought Valam up-to-date. Father Jacob's account was very well spoken, which was a big surprise, mostly to himself, because of the confusion in his thoughts.

Valam was slow to respond as Jacob finished, and Jacob had not expected, nor wanted Valam to reply to his words. Nevertheless, Valam spoke. Sorrow overshadowed his words, which would hang heavy on all who were present for a long time to come. After he finished, Valam returned above decks; there was too much to be done to allow a delay to mull over past events.

Shortly after Valam left, Captain Mikhal knocked on the cabin door and entered. The captain remained very official as he walked in and announced that the flagman was already sending orders to the other ships. By his estimate, if they hurried, the camp, which included the new arrivals and many supplies, could be fully organized by nightfall.

Seth stopped Father Jacob, who was about to leave the room,

after Captain Mikhal departed. Seth understood much more than Jacob did about Valam's current situation; a number of pressing matters were on Valam's shoulders already and Seth also knew enough about Jacob to say the right words to calm him. "It was not your fault, Father Jacob. You said the right things. He will accept it. Give him some time. I felt the things he did not say."

"You, Brother Seth, are a very wise man," said Father Jacob, as the despair began to leave his eyes.

"Yes, but I know another wiser," replied Seth. "Come, I have someone I would really like to introduce you to. I think you and he will have a lot in common."

Seth introduced Father Jacob to Teren, Tsandra, and lastly Liyan. He was right—Liyan and Father Jacob were very much alike. He could feel questions bubbling through the father's mind as the three talked. Momentarily, Seth's thoughts roamed to Valam, who had gone to the bow of the ship where only the wind in his face was a companion.

Valam stayed there for a long time watching the waves roll into the ship and feeling the swaying of the boat beneath his feet. He contemplated numerous things before he finally rejoined his friends, but most importantly he said a few long overdue words to someone who was gone. Afterwards he felt much the better for saying those words.

Chapter Eleven

High, fortified walls of stone rose before them, looming greater with each step. Even on their horses, the travelers looked minuscule compared to the heights of the peaks; the mighty oaks even paled in comparison. Their minds were filled with wonder, even though some had seen the guarded fortress before.

Noman reminded them that it was more an outcropping of rock, a mountain, than a man-made structure, but awe still marked their expressions as they passed within the city gates. The only requirement for passage was a token, an offering that spoke more even than gold to those who dwelled within the city's walls. All had readily given up their armaments without a word of protest. Most had heard rumors of the penalty for not doing so, and Noman ensured that they heard them again as fact, so when they were requested to relinquish their arms, they did so quickly out of fear more than anything else.

The horses and carriages were deposited at a livery that was tucked just inside the walls. No animals were allowed into the city streets, another rule that none challenged. The only good law they fell under was the hood drawn close to Adrina's face, and the cloak attached, which dropped to her ankles. A woman's flesh could beguile the eyes of the beholder, and that was an intolerable insult. Concealment at this point was what they had planned for Adrina all along, and the cloak made it all the easier.

Noman carefully reminded them of the rules, begging them to insure that no one broke any of them. They quickly made for the closest inn. Noman also made sure that everyone knew why they were here, telling them that although the disadvantages seemed to outweigh the advantages, a great deal could be gained, chief among which was information.

The first inn they came upon was unremarkable in all respects from the outside, a fact that Xith highly approved. The inside was plain and clear, with a short staircase at either end of a long, almost oval-shaped hall. The atmosphere was dim but well aired, the kind of place they could feel right at home in, Xith especially.

As it was still very early in the day, the inn was mostly empty save for the inn-keeper and a single man servant, who was quick to show them to their respective rooms following the payment of a small retainer. The rooms were small and quite cramped with furniture, each having two beds, a washstand, standing closets, which were unusual. Most surprising was the table with four chairs, rarely seen in an inn in the kingdom.

The rooms had a stagnant odor of heavy smoke or possibly perfume that had been around for a long time. Since the innkeeper had only afforded them four rooms, several cots were brought in and crowded the tiny spaces, eliminating any hope of movement. This might have been deliberate. If they had no area to relax in they would probably use the inn's bar all the more. Strangers did not fare well in the eyes of the populace, but their money was never refused.

Xith wondered if they would have received better accommodations if he told the innkeeper that they planned to spend a goodly amount of time partaking of his ale. This was part of their plan, for there was no better place to gather information. Xith, Noman, and Nijal requested that Amir and Adrina wait upstairs and that Shchander and his men proceed to the tavern below while they went to have a look about the city.

Noman would have preferred Amir at his side, but he understood Xith's choice and accepted it as a fair one. The best place for Amir was beside Adrina. They need not fear for her safety while they were gone. Nijal was very quick to his feet and out the door, for he expected Amir to object.

The structures they passed along the city streets were in heavy contrast to the high stone walls surrounding them. Largely constructed of wood with little stone, they seemed an oddity. The levels spiraling up around them were also unusual and a masterful feat of architecture.

As the three strode deep into the city's center, the area over their heads began to look cramped. The upper levels of the buildings were connected by a series of interconnecting suspended bridges with some structures having as many as ten or more such bridges leading from their upper floors. Xith explained to Nijal that this was because the walls of the city had been constructed very long ago, and any room for expansion along the city's avenues had been used up centuries ago. The only direction that remained to build was up, an art the residents had perfected through the ages.

Noman looked for a shop that had long been on the second floor of the district they now wandered through. To get to the second level, they had to take a short cut through several stores connected at street level. This brought them to a staircase that opened to another shop on the second level, which finally carried them out to a bridge crossing.

Nijal took Noman's sudden halt midway across the bridge as a sign that it was okay to look about. He watched the people wander the streets below; most were tall and stout, even the women, or at least those he thought were women because of the cloaks wrapped tightly around them. He noticed that most of the people greeted each other with a bleak grimace on their faces, which changed to an expressionless mask afterwards.

Xith quickly pulled Nijal across the bridge and into an adjacent shop, which turned out to be a residence. They left hurriedly. "I thought you knew where you were going!" hissed Xith.

"It has been some time; give me a moment," said Noman.

They crisscrossed back and forth along the avenue, moving in and out of many different places, ending up several blocks from where they started, but Noman assured Xith that this was the corner he had been seeking. The new levels of the ever changing city had just thrown him off, that's all. Their confused actions brought much attention to their movements, and many shopkeepers and residents stared at them from their doorways.

The place they stood in front of looked more like someone's home than a shop of any sort. It was completely dark from the outside, and no sign hung above its door. It appeared rather deserted. Noman tried the door, which gingerly opened at his touch, and he urged Xith and Nijal to step inside speedily.

There was no light in the room save that which poured in from around the frame of the door. It took some time for their eyes to adjust to the darkness. As their eyes adjusted, they noticed that the room was completely empty, void of all furniture or sign of inhabitation.

"Nothing!" said Nijal, "Let's leave."

"Not just yet," said Noman, "this is the place we were looking for."

"But it's empty."

"Only by appearances."

Noman entered a corridor that Nijal had not seen until the other stepped into it. He then opened a door and deep amber light issued forth, for which Nijal was very thankful. Nijal turned to talk to Xith, but Xith was not there. "Come on, hurry!" whispered Noman to Nijal. Hesitantly, Nijal followed.

The room they walked into was extremely large but was as cluttered as their rooms at the inn. Nijal thought to himself that the owner would do well to move some of these things into the empty space he had been standing in moments before. At the end of a long, narrow table sat an old man bent with the weight of many years. The light came from a single lantern on a table beside him.

Noman pulled a long-handled dagger from his cloak, the likes of which Nijal had never seen. The blade was twisted from the tip to the hilt and inlaid with fine workmanship; an animal of sorts appeared on one side and a man on the other. Nijal saw this only because he now held the dagger in his own hand, as Noman handed it to him.

"Be true on your mark," whispered Noman, "you only have one chance."

"You mean, throw it?"

"Yes, but do not miss."

"Kill him?"

"Yes, of course."

Nijal was confused at best, but proceeded as Noman instructed. The tip of the blade felt cold in his hands as he touched it. He drew his arm back straight and precise, taking in a deep breath, and holding it as he released. The blade fell end over end, directly on target, just as Nijal intended.

Nijal saw the dagger touch the man's head just between the eyes where he aimed it, but it went no further. The man raised his eyes from the tome he read as if impatient for having been disturbed. "Very peculiar way of greeting," rolled the words from the old man's tongue in a slow, drawn-out drawl.

"Yes, very peculiar indeed," replied Noman, adding after a short silence, "just returning the favor."

"Still holding on to that after such a long time, eh?"

"The past is often all we have."

"Yes, yes it is," said the man, indicating they should sit.

"Where is Xith?" asked Nijal quietly.

"He will return shortly."

"Has it come so quickly?"

"Nay, it has not been quick," said Noman, "I believe you still owe me one favor."

"Yes, the last," spoke the old man lightly.

"You know I would not ask if the need were not great."

"Old friend, you least of all need explain yourself. Talk, and I will listen."

Many words long and wise passed across Noman's lips in the hours that followed. Nijal mostly sat and listened, eyes wide with wonder at the re-telling. He also learned many things, and a great many things suddenly became clear to him.

Xith came back shortly after Noman came to the end and returned to the present. The old one's face lit up as Xith entered the room and crossed it to sit beside Noman. During his absence, Xith had acquired and filled a satchel. Something within had a heavy sweet aroma, which now rose and lingered just above the table, seemingly within reach of their watering tongues.

"Is it clear now?" asked the old one of Xith.

"I did not see it until it was beneath my nose, but as we came inside, I knew it could only be your house. You said one day I would meet him, and until a short while ago I did not believe you. And here you sit as if waiting."

"I was. Now, for me it is complete," said the man, adding after a lengthy break, "with the last, of course." He spread his lips to form a toothless smile. "You were always the obstinate one, weren't you?"

"That I was, but I remembered my promise," said Xith, drawing a small package from his satchel. Nijal passed it on, and the old man snatched it up, setting it on the corner of the table beside him as if it were gold, where it lay unopened.

He cleared his voice, deep and harsh, vibrating the air in the room. And then there was silence while he stopped, apparently engrossed in thought. "The time approaches although you see it not. Its shadows are far reaching and some already think it has arrived, but alas it has not. You will mark the time beyond it, when your eyes are once again filled with sight." The last sentence had been directed entirely at Noman, which was very clear to those who watched. His eyes grew distant and unfocused, and his face grew pale.

Nijal could no longer comprehend the words. As he strained to hear them, only bits and pieces carried through to his consciousness. Puzzled and frustrated, he mulled over each sound he perceived, but soon all understanding was beyond him. Only a single fragment of all that followed remained in his mind as the sound of words came to a halt. "The dragons are with her."

"Until the next, Y'sat," called out Xith as he, Nijal, and Noman departed.

"Are we returning to the inn?" asked Nijal.

"No, we have one more stop. Stay close," chided Xith.

After returning through the maze of shops, bridges, and buildings, they found themselves back on the ground level and a short time later they left the center of the city behind. The wall now loomed overhead, and it blocked out the last of the late-day sun, so now they wandered through the shadows, which for Nijal was not a comforting fact.

The dwellings they passed along and sometimes through, up and around, were newer; and construction, almost entirely upward, was ongoing. It was apparent to Nijal that both Xith and

Noman were looking for a place he suspected they had never been to before. As far as he could tell, they probably only knew it by name, or even face, if it were a person they sought.

They walked until only a single street stood between them and the northernmost part of the wall. The narrow byroad ran east to west and was obviously losing the fight to maintain a distance between the buildings and the wall, both of which appeared to be closing in on it. At the far easterly corner, a thin tapering stair circled its way up the wall, the only stair they had seen in the whole of the wall.

Xith smiled as he saw the stair and turned almost mid-step, taking a bearing on it and the wall. Directly in front of him was a small alleyway. Two shops down, out of the darkness, shone a lantern. Below it, hung a little wooden sign with a picture of a clenched fist.

Unlike the cramped alleyways that led to the alehouse, the Clenched-Fist was quite spacious and resounded with laughter and song, which took Nijal completely by surprise. Xith pushed Nijal to the fore, and so he entered first, followed by Xith and then Noman.

The bar was crowded with people drinking and singing, but Xith steered Nijal to a dark, dingy back room, where amidst the gloom sat a group of men who did not appear to notice them. Their eyes were fixed on the wall at the far end of the room and a man who stood with a set of knives in his hand. On the wall was a target of sorts, where after much deliberation and calculation, the man directed his blades.

Nijal snickered and whispered to Xith, "I could do better

than that," words that he would soon regret as Xith replied, "That is what we hoped."

"Why me?" asked Nijal.

"We, my friend, are in need of a little pocket money, and you need the practice."

"This is for money?"

"What else would it be for?"

Nijal knew right then that he was in for a long evening. "But I don't even know the rules."

"All the better," retorted Xith, "all the better."

"But, but—"

"Listen closely. Here are the rules; they are quite simple. There are three marks, the hands, left and right, and the head. If you lead, you pick the mark; if you follow, you must make the same marks as the opponent. You have three blades. Aim for the center of each mark; beware the outstretched fingers; how hard can that be?"

Xith left out most of the details in the rules, but Nijal soon caught on as he watched. "Are you ready?" asked Xith and before Nijal could answer, Xith raised his wager to the board. A murmur rose as he placed the gold piece down beside the one who stood thus far undefeated.

"You little man?" boomed a loud voice.

Xith wavered his head, and pointed to Nijal. Nijal sank in his chair under the stern gaze he quickly received. The man smiled and said, "Watch, and Pilio will show you how it's done."

Pilio stood stiffly, meticulously aligning himself with the target. After much deliberation, he delivered his first knife nicely, center right hand. He followed through with a second to the head, and the last to the left hand. His blades were all directly centered in their respective places.

Nijal still had to hold back a laugh as he watched Pilio. He looked as if he were under severe strain as he took aim, and his relief came only when all three knives had left his hand. He weighed each dagger in his hand before he started. He found it odd that all three were of different weights, another fact that Xith had obviously neglected to tell him. The differences in weight made it more difficult to follow through with aim and delivery.

To some degree, Nijal now understood Pilio's hesitation. He also considered that now it would be more difficult for him to be centered on target, as the blades were still in the target. He calculated his first choice. He considered a long time before he released the first, but it held true to its destination. After a quick adjustment for weight and positioning, he threw the last two. His shots, although nice and clean within the target, were not as centered as his competitor, and Pilio quickly claimed his prize.

"Again," said Xith, this time putting two gold coins on the table. Pilio accepted the offer without thought; he would take a fool's money any time. His next three shots, to the surprise of the onlookers, were all to the right hand, and were nicely packed around the center point of the palm. Nijal tossed a stern look to Xith; there was no way he could match or even win. He was left with little space in which to place his blades, but he tried. Two to the center, and one to the outside, which cost Xith his gold.

Pilio's grin broadened as he plucked up the gold and tucked it away into his purse, a small leather satchel tucked into his belt at his side. Noman said nothing so far, but he watched intensely. Xith again placed two gold coins for a bet.

Nijal watched Pilio with grave concern as he, with great care, placed his marks on the target, center, left, and right. "Relax," soothed Noman as Nijal paced the floor. Nijal's first knife, although slightly off center was placed well. He hesitated on the second, considering the blade in his hand. The second glided from his hand, landing fair, but the third fell dead center, and to his surprise he won, which he only knew because of the dejected look on Pilio's face.

With a slightly red face, Pilio gave up the gold coins, and Xith readily accepted. Nijal paused, as he had never been first and had to think about where to begin. Pilio stopped Nijal a moment and traded sets of knives with him. Although confused, Nijal accepted, giving his blades back to Pilio.

The balance of the new daggers was completely different from those that Nijal previously used, causing him to delay as he considered each separately. Satisfied, Nijal began again. The wins and losses shifted back and forth for a long while with neither side clearly claiming victory, although Pilio's purse was visibly shrunken. Xith tossed in a "Good, good!" now and again, but he, like Noman, was mostly quiet.

Nijal was growing quite pleased with his performance as the night drew on. His lack of common sense and his vanity cost him the next two matches, but he won the third quite skillfully with three neatly thrown scores. He winked at Pilio as he exchanged blades with him, taking careful pace from the target. He also cast a wink towards Xith and Noman as he cast his first knife.

The wink cost him dearly, for he twitched just as the blade released from his fingers. Pilio's eyes went wide as the tip struck one of the outstretched fingers of the left hand. Suddenly the room filled with the noise of people shifting heavily in their chairs or coughing. Nijal smiled at Xith and turned to Pilio and shrugged his shoulders. Xith was clearly worried and angry, but he walked over to where Nijal stood and calmly said to him in a low tone, "You must get two more fingers of the left hand. Do not miss."

"Or what?" whispered Nijal in jest.

"Just do it!" snapped Xith, greatly displeased.

Nijal stared at Xith as he walked away and retook his place beside Noman. The many eyes fixed upon him, quietly watching, bore heavily upon him. He didn't understand what he had done, but he knew when to listen to Xith. For a very long time, he stood contemplating the dagger in his hand and the target before him. Xith took in a deep breath as the second dagger struck the middle finger.

As Nijal stood poised with the third dagger, he could feel the room stop with him as if everyone waited to draw in a breath. He closed his eyes; the air was charged about him as he heavily breathed it in. He opened his eyes and fixed on the target, drawing his hand back slowly, releasing only after he calculated the balance of the blade in his hand. "Yes!" he cried as it hit. Xith shook his head at Nijal, who still did not understand the gravity of his situation.

Pilio was more tedious and cautious than ever as he stood at the ready. He insured the placement of his feet just behind the line, but then he had to insure the validity of the line again, so he paced it off and then repositioned himself. The whole process was long and very meticulous. The joyful expression had long since left Pilio's face. He closed his eyes in relief as the first took the index finger of the right hand cleanly on mark.

Pilio paced back and forth as he concentrated on his next mark. He even went so far as to measure the balance of the dagger on the tip of his finger and to check the movement of the air within the room. All of a sudden, he stopped and placed the two remaining daggers he held onto the table, rubbing his sweaty palms until they were dry. Then, after flexing his fingers and cracking each knuckle, he picked up only one of the daggers, moving slowly and methodically back into his stance.

His face showed displeasure as the knife tumbled from his fingertips, but it hit its mark, and he sighed deeply in relief. He was growing visibly nervous as he placed the last blade carefully in his hand, also insuring its balance before he drew his arm back and released it. The entire process took the better part of a quarter of an hour.

Astonished as it struck, Pilio rushed to the board to check, as did several onlookers. The tip of the knife had struck directly on the line of the third finger. Being an honest man, the only virtue he held to, Pilio accepted his loss.

Pilio pulled the blade from the target and handed it to Nijal, saying, "I didn't mean to offend. Take whichever one you like." Pilio placed his hands outstretched onto the table. Xith jumped up from his chair and ran towards the two, afraid of what Nijal would do. "We will be quite satisfied with quadruple our original wager."

"Quadruple?" asked Pilio, raising his quivering voice high.

"Quadruple," replied Xith.

Pilio sighed, hurriedly pulled from his purse a handful of gold, and passed it to Nijal. He thought the sum was a very fair amount, given the circumstances. "Good match, master," said Pilio. Xith immediately took Nijal away. The three of them hurriedly left the Clenched-Fist.

A little confused and slightly hurt, Nijal turned to Xith and said, "I didn't know."

"Never mind," returned Xith.

Noman's response was somewhat gentler than Xith's and he made a valid point. Xith had not told Nijal all the rules of the game. "I think he did well, quite well, all things considered."

Chapter Twelve

Chancellor Volnej detached himself from the other six. He was alone, pacing heavily across the floor. Many thoughts weighed on his mind: the kingdom was without council, without an heir, and soon to be without a capital. He had watched the keepers fall, the council fall, the priests of the Father fall, noble hearted men fall. His heart could not endure all the pain, nor could his mind.

He was too weary and old to have the will to go on a prolonged journey of any sort, let alone try to escape. He would only slow the others down and surely cause their capture. His mind was resolved; he would stay in Imtal. In his own way he could not stand to leave it nor could he abide to see it fall, but he was sure that he must stay.

The venerable chancellor thought of a way to insure that the others would leave him. He thought about it as he listened to them. He had served king and prince and long-ago queen while on the high council. He considered his life to have been very fulfilled and fruitful, but now he saw only an ending before him. As he approached the others, it was Calyin who understood the message upon his face first and she begged him to come with them, but his mind was sternly set.

"With three, we are seven," whispered Calyin as she held his hand firmly.

"No, that is not true. I do not believe I was included in those words. In fact, I am almost positive."

"I think the chancellor is correct," said Swordmaster Timmer. "I also believe my place is here."

"As do I. We stay!" said Captain Brodst.

"No, Captain Brodst, your fate is with them; of this I am also sure. Listen to an old man, who is many years your elder speak to you with wisdom."

"Do not worry," said Timmer, moving towards the chancellor. Timmer also understood the reasons Volnej thought it best to stay. His sword arm was not what it used to be, and if a real fight came, they would not survive it. They needed speed, and on foot they did not need old men to slow them down. "I will take care of Chancellor Volnej. We will find a way through this, but you, my friends, must go. I think together we can get you past the city gates, but beyond it there will just be the five of you, as it was meant to be."

Lord Serant's voice turned icy cold as he stared at Captain Brodst; he could tell that the captain still was not convinced that he should go. "I have never fully accounted what occurred in the square after the struggle and the mysterious two who appeared before us wearing faces very dear to our hearts. I have not even spoken fully of this to Calyin, my beloved wife, for he bade me speak to none until the time had come when the truth could be prolonged no more. But in fact, few ever saw the face of the stranger. Of those they were mostly Geoffrey and his men, who are now twice indebted to the one, if I am correct."

Geoffrey lowered his head and then raised it.

"The remainder who saw him are gone save a few of us here at this very moment. I know questions lie in your minds as they do in mine, and I am also afraid that in truth I know little more than Lord Geoffrey, but I believed then and I wholly and firmly believe now the words that the one called Noman spoke to me. He said, 'Our paths are coming to an end and a meeting, and our time is at an end and a beginning.' He spoke of many things quickly and carefully, for he wanted me to remember in full detail when the time came, if it came; but he had little time to tarry. He told me that none would question what they had seen on the square that day beyond what I offered, and no one has. He told me the names of the three I would journey away from the darkness with, and of that I had my doubts, for how could anyone hold the future so well in their hands and still not know it in its entirety? But now the faces stand before me in an hour of grave peril. Geoffrey, Midori, and Captain Brodst."

Calyin raised her eyes as if wondering if she had been mentioned.

"Yes, my dear, he also said he saw a hand clasped in mine, but not a face and that is you. So you see, Captain Brodst, you must come. Your fate lies with us."

"What of the seven the others spoke of?"

"Of this, I am sure. It will be revealed to us all in good time. Come, we have delayed far too long."

Turmoil, the thing they counted on to make their escape possible, was decreasing. The ebbing of the sounds of battle and the emptiness of the halls and courtyards told them this. Although they were still using obscure corridors and rooms, they still expected to meet some resistance as they made their way; however, up to now they found none. They hid themselves some 200 feet from the rear wall of the palace, staring in disbelief at the open, unoccupied gate.

"There is some trick about. There must be," whispered Lord Serant.

"I do not believe so," replied Volnej.

"I side with Lord Serant. I do not trust it, but we have no choice but to move forward and soon," added Geoffrey.

"Let's go!" said Midori moving from their guarded spot. Lord Serant put out his arm to halt her. "Wait," bade Serant. He squinted to the far corner tower. "There, do you see it," he said pointing.

"I'll be," said Geoffrey as he also caught a glimpse of the forms hiding in the shadows.

"How do we get past?" asked Captain Brodst, considering the options himself as he asked the question.

"I see two options: run or take them out."

"I'll vote on running," quickly stated Timmer, even though he had the least chance of success for such a measure.

"Surely there are more in waiting. I say we find another way."

"I do not believe we have the time. Timmer, Volnej, and Geoffrey, you take the right, and we three will take the left. Captain Brodst, your job is to get their attention."

"And then what?" whispered Captain Brodst.

"Don't worry; I trust your judgment. We'll follow."

"Thanks, thanks a lot!" muttered Brodst as he crept carefully away from the wall. The others behind him split into two groups as Lord Serant had requested, one moving left and the other right. The captain counted his blessings; at least he knew the back wall better than the others. Stairs stood in each of the towers at either end of the wall with two more narrow staircases on either side of the gates within the guardhouses.

Captain Brodst was very careful of the sound of his footfalls on the hard-surfaced stairs, but even so the rock carried an echo upward. He was fortunate to know exactly what lay around each turn, and as he passed the last stair, he stopped. He shrank down to all fours and peered around the corner, looking in both directions. He noted two sentries to the left and several more far to the right.

He watched them for a time, hoping the others were doing likewise before they swept forward. One of the guards, a tall, lanky-looking fellow clad in a loosely fitting robe with a heavy mailed suit beneath, was signaling to someone in the square opposite the palace walls. "Damn it," cursed Brodst. The man fell as he was clubbed from behind. His companion was quick to follow him.

Captain Brodst ran forward, still bent over, coming up behind one of those to the right. Before he reached him, Geoffrey had already waylaid his companion and the man was about to scream, but Brodst clipped his tongue just in time. Captain Brodst pulled Geoffrey down behind the wall, signaling for the other two to do likewise.

"What is it?" asked Geoffrey.

"In the square there are more. Pray that they did not see your foolishness."

"We had to act," said Geoffrey, but as he turned back, the captain was gone. He had already crept back towards Lord Serant. Fortunately, Lord Serant had the good sense to crouch down after the successful attack. Captain Brodst whispered the news to him, "There are others in the square."

"Yes, I know," replied Lord Serant.

"Fool, then why did you stand and take him."

"The sentry below had turned his back to us."

Captain Brodst swallowed any further words. He knew Serant wasn't a fool, so he should have known better than to think he would be careless in so grave a matter. He thought to offer an apology, but Lord Serant had already turned to other matters.

"We were not seen, I am sure," spoke Geoffrey as he reached the place where Captain Brodst perched, peering over the wall ever so slightly.

"Good, good. Timmer, Volnej?"

"They watch the stairs at the tower and the guardhouse."

"Come, we must be swift. Two more approach," said Lord Serant, springing to action. He carried everyone with him as he made for the place Timmer watched. Serant issued hurried orders; he supposed that two men were positioned on either side of the gate. Geoffrey and Timmer would take them out. He would go straight for the one who stood in the center of the square. He assumed that that one was the leader, and was the one he had seen signaling the others. Volnej was to make certain that Calyin and Midori reached the far side of the square and the alleyway beyond. And Captain Brodst had the two who approached from the palace proper; he was to take them out as he saw fit, only doing so if it became necessary.

As Serant reached the bottom landing, he stopped firm, waiting for Geoffrey and Timmer to pass him before he began to move again, meanwhile drawing his sword and a small blade. He touched the two on the shoulder as they passed, so instructing them to halt. He waited for the one to turn his back to him and as he did, Lord Serant whispered, "Go!"

Lord Serant sprinted across the square, his feet softly striking the stones. His boots lay discarded some distance away. His blade was swift and true as he released it from his hand, dropping the man where he stood. His sword soon followed up to insure that the man was dead. He whispered in his mind as he did so, "Fool, soft leather does little to protect you in battle. Death has found you."

Lord Serant carefully scanned the area around the square in a wide circle. He saw Calyin and the other two reach the safety of the dark alley. Timmer and Geoffrey had felled their opponents and were also on their way to hiding. Only Captain Brodst was absent. "Come on," whispered Serant under his breath. He turned nervously, pausing only to take in the surrounding shadows again. "Come on," he thought again.

"Yes," struck his mind as he saw the captain's form racing towards him. He retrieved his dagger and relieved the dead one of his blade while he waited for Captain Brodst to catch up to him; then the two crept off across the square.

From the shadows of many alleys, byways, and small paths

the seven stole from the city center toward the postern gates on the lower east side, a direction that Lord Serant hoped would not be as closely watched as the others, since it was not an obvious exit. It had been sealed for decades; furthermore, it lay just off the lower market square in plain view.

Lord Serant was pleased to see that Calyin and Midori had wisely collected several blades for their own use, so he stashed at his own side the short sword he had obtained; an extra blade would always come in handy. The streets were mostly empty, which did not surprise Lord Serant. His heart sorrowed for the citizens of Imtal, whom he could not protect from King Jarom's greedy hands, but he vowed to return and amend the situation at the first opportunity. Under other circumstances, he would have thought his deeds cowardly, and cowardice did not sit well with him. But for now, in view of what he had seen, he considered his actions a tactical, necessary retreat.

Sore bodies carried them and weary legs moved tired feet, but their minds pushed them on beyond their limits. Soon they found themselves on the edge of a small deserted marketplace. Lord Serant marked the progress of the sun as he planned their movements. They would move just after dusk; the wait would not be long. All things considered, he thought this day was the longest of his life. It seemed to him that the sun fought to linger in the skies overhead to prevent darkness from arriving.

The minutes, or hours, of waiting seemed to go on forever, but darkness eventually began to fall. The air around them had a peaceful silence as it had since their arrival. The beating of their hearts seemed to echo around them. Their breaths became great bellows and the shifting of their feet a blade on a grindstone. Eyes flickered nervously back and forth, up and down, ever watching.

"Are you sure you know how to open this?" whispered Brodst to Serant.

"I am sure," replied Calyin, speaking before Lord Serant could reply. "A certain boy I knew long ago had taken a fancy to this very exit, or entrance rather—" Her voice died on the last words, and no one heard them save for Serant who was directly beside her.

"Yes, he did show me," he softly whispered into Calyin's ear; his voice was also saddened. "With luck he will return, though I hope not soon. The goings-on would shrivel his heart and pluck out his eyes."

The sound of horses' hooves froze his heart and his lips. Everyone drew tight against the wall, withdrawing into the gray shadows as best they could. Two horsemen broke into the square directly across from their position, coming straight for them. Serant edged back along the shadows, but he held firm for a time, hoping the riders would not come near.

The clatter of several pairs of hooves against hard rock carried loudly to their listening ears. The two riders seemed to circle the square two or three times as if searching. Once or twice Brodst and Serant perceived eyes on them, but then as swiftly as the two appeared, they were gone. The sound of their retreat echoed for a long time before it faded away. Lord Serant slumped against the wall and sank to his knees in relief; they would wait for a short time before they would go for the wall and escape beyond it. He hoped the night would be very dark.

In a tiny cleft hidden three bricks high and two bricks in along the high stone wall, lay the gate key, where it had lain now for many years. Lord Serant breathed deeply and flashed its form back to the others who yet waited in the shadows. The night was as dark as he would have hoped; stars peeked in and out of light cloud cover and a twinkle of brass caught Captain Brodst's eye. He bade the others to follow his lead into the square.

One by one they crossed the square to the dark recesses by the wall. Geoffrey was the last to leave the alley, his methodical gait, though scarcely audible, grew closer. Five waited patiently for his arrival. Timmer remained where he was; this was the end of his journey this day. The chancellor had only left his side to insure that the gate was secured before the two made their retreat, which would be separate from the others. The chancellor and Timmer had business elsewhere within the city, and not beyond it. Lord Serant fiddled with the key in his hand, waiting to release the latch when all was clear.

A shrill noise brought cold shivers. Geoffrey slumped flat against cool stone, lying motionless, waiting to insure that movement was safe. The noise passed, as sounds in the dark often do, and Geoffrey rose to his knees and crept away. He did not relax until Serant touched his shoulder reassuringly. "All is well," he whispered.

Lord Serant touched key to keyhole and turned it; after a slight hesitation and a little resistance, the old lock released and with a creak the gate opened. He did not dare to push it open more than a foot, fearing that the noise of the old hinges would surely rouse someone's attention. Serant was the first to slip beyond the city's walls and into the breezes of the night. Here Volnej parted with the others. Good-byes were hurried and speechless, as there was nothing more to be said, and their voices need not be heard.

Chapter Thirteen

Hours before the sun rose, the camp was a jumble of activity. Renewed hope and faith filled the thoughts of many. Prince Valam had returned at long last. They had enough supplies to carry them through the cold that lay ahead, and now they were ready to train for the coming challenge with all their hearts, more than ever before.

Seth regarded Liyan with inquiring eyes. There was something bothering Liyan, but he could not tell what. As he watched Liyan, he paced back and forth, and every now and again, he would glance out the small opening at the front of the tent to note the weather.

Several hours past first light, a messenger arrived with a summons for them. They were to meet the others in the command tent. The messenger said that Prince Valam was already anxiously awaiting their arrival. The two followed the messenger back towards the center of the camp and then circled off towards the command tent.

By the time Seth and Liyan arrived, almost everyone was already present and seated around the conference table, which was strewn with scrolls and maps, and even the remnants of several breakfasts, which were being cleared away as they entered. Seth wasn't surprised to find that Teren had already returned to the plains and his watch. He could tell that Teren had longed to be alone and away from past memories.

Tsandra sat smugly beside Cagan, and the two were engrossed in conversation. Evgej, Valam, and Father Jacob had withdrawn to a quiet corner away from the confusion at the center table. Captain Mikhal and several other men that Seth did not know were seated around the center table although Seth did not see the one called Danyel'.

Valam quickly returned when he noticed that Seth was present. He had been awaiting Seth and Liyan's arrival. Just as they were about to begin and the room grew quiet, several men hurried in and took their seats, apologizing for their tardiness. Valam did an account of who was present and who was still unaccounted for. Only Danyel' was still missing. He dispatched another runner to find him.

The room began to grow restless after a ten minute wait with no sign of Danyel'. Captain Mikhal grew visibly flushed as the lieutenant was his responsibility, so it became his fault that Danyel' was absent. After waiting several more minutes, Valam decided to begin without him even though he had counted on the other's presence.

Introductions were first, which Valam carried out at length, hoping Danyel' would arrive before he finished, but Danyel' did not. Valam went through a long list of names, titles and positions, adhering to the elaborate way Seth's people formally announced themselves. He started off with Liyan, and ended with Cagan.

Tsandra was annoyed, for he had saved her for second to last, and she thought he was going to rank her last. Afterwards, he similarly announced those from the kingdom, saving the six lieutenants for last, and with side consultation from Captain Mikhal he made it through their names without error.

He finished and took his place at the table, marking each of the names in his mind, associating each with something that would stick in his memory and help him recall the name. Lieutenant Willam had piercing eyes of coal that held a hint of sparkle, perhaps a touch of blue or maybe it was just the reflection of the light. Pavil had a long wispy mustache and a stunted goatee. He stopped at Eran for a time, listening to what Father Jacob was saying and accidentally skipped to Tae, whose auburn locks were immediately distinctive, and then he backed up to Eran. He didn't really note anything that he could mark in his thoughts, so he went on. His eyes fell on Tae again. He stumbled once more over the face, which he had seen often at Quashan', but the name did not jump out at him, and he wondered why. S'tryil was another easy one, for he was the bladesmen to whom the prince and the entire kingdom was deeply indebted. Plus if he recalled correctly he had known a Lord S'tryil in his youth, perhaps the lieutenant's father. He would have to talk with S'tryil about that later.

Valam smiled as Father Jacob's words sparked his memory. Redcliff, that's the name, he thought, and he cast a sidelong glance at Tae although he couldn't quite recall how the nickname had come about. The last one Valam knew well; he did not need anything to recall the name. Ylsa had served directly under

Captain Evgej when he had been a mere swordmaster third-class, and she had helped him, in fact, to attain the rank of swordmaster first-class. The rank of captain had come much later, of course, and only recently, but she was also a mystery to him, as Evgej had been until a short time ago. "Was it a short time?" thought Valam to himself. In all actuality it seemed so very long ago that the two of them and Seth had been together in the Belyj forest.

The weather outside turned severe as if on cue as Father Jacob raised the topic, discussing Liyan's concerns at length. Jacob cast a dreary sidelong stare at the flakes of snow falling just beyond his touch. Brother Liyan was correct—this odd season was full upon them, as was readily apparent.

Father Jacob paused only shortly, and then returned to full eloquent speech, laden with elaborate words, trying firmly to make his point, which he had considered thoroughly during many long and empty nights. He had been all set for a return trip to the kingdom and was rather disappointed at the turn of events. At long last, Jacob concluded and offered the floor to Valam, who was slow to draw on the cue offered him.

Valam had only briefly returned from his reverie and stood, as a commotion outside caused him to stop cold on his first word. He was the first to go to the door and first to hear the excited runner's message. "Riders from the north." Valam came to attention quickly. "How many?"

"Lieutenant Danyel' did not say, sire."

"Danyel'—where are Lieutenant Danyel' and his men?"

The runner pointed to the North, "Just beyond the first hill; they wait."

"Is he mad?" asked Valam aloud, although he had meant only to think it.

The runner nodded courteously and begged graciously to be dismissed, which Valam did without second thought. Valam's face grew pale as he retreated back into the tent and spread the news. He did not delay to run toward the far northerly side of the camp, clutching his sword. As he approached, he saw nothing but a rather large commotion spreading like wildfire around Danyel', who was mounted.

His eyes scanned the distance, but he saw nothing. He called out to the lieutenant, but his words were drowned amidst many voices. He waited until he was at the lieutenant's side to gain his attention. He did not have to speak, for the men quickly made a path for him to Danyel'; it was done without words and without hesitation. The men held him in extreme reverence since his return, even beyond that which his office normally rendered him.

"My prince, you have come. I give thanks," spoke Danyel', echoing his men's respect for Valam.

"What is it?"

"Listen."

Danyel' did not have to ask for silence. It followed as if Valam had ordered it. Valam listened, but he could hear nothing. "Wait," offered Danyel', "put your ear to the ground; it will tell."

Valam put his ear against the hard ground and listened. At first he heard nothing, but soon afterwards a faint rumbling sound rose to his ears. "How far away are they?"

"A good ten miles, but they come, sire."

"Can you tell how many?"

"My prince, it is a large group or the thunder would not carry such a distance. I would guess hundreds or more."

"Please part with the niceties," spoke Valam, "I am no king," and responding with the humbleness of Seth's people, a way which he had grown accustomed to and now preferred, he said, "I am the governor of South Province, son of Andrew, King of the Great Kingdom, this is true, which does make me a prince, but no more. I am very honored by your words and your reverence, but if such a tribute is to be paid to me, let it be earned in the field of battle and nowhere else."

In so saying, he endeared himself even more to those who listened. His voice became silent as he put all his attention on a distant point. Seth, Cagan and Evgej soon arrived, and after a short explanation, they waited, poised. Behind them the camp roused, as if to battle.

Seth considered the possibility that those approaching did not yet know of their presence, and his thoughts could possibly give that away to them if he reached out, so he would be silent until the force was close at hand.

Liyan was troubled; he watched quietly, whispering his thoughts only to Seth's mind. Behind him, Tsandra stood poised defiantly beside her mount, and forming behind her were those of her order, who gathered at her summons. Cagan and Evgej, who now stood to Valam's left and Seth's right, waited also.

Evgej, who had been afraid of the seas and very often seasick on their journey to the Eastern Reaches, missed the water and the craft of his forefathers whom he had long ago forsaken. He had never told Cagan that his father was a shipbuilder and that his father had been the one to build the ship for him, the one the rocks and sea had lain to rest. Evgej cut off the memories, thinking them odd for a time when his hand played along the hilt of his sword in waiting.

The uncomfortable waiting ended as a herald rose to their thoughts and to their hearts like the sound of a bugle in triumph. The will of Teren entered the minds of all who stood waiting. He told them he carried with him a band of mountaineers or so he named them, those he considered to be of his order, which was not that of the brown.

Teren's companions, all strongly built for elves, looked to be worthy adversaries in the trials that lay ahead. They, like Teren, lived on the Great Plains and roamed its vast span, changing their place of dwelling like the wind and with the seasons. Most often, or so Teren explained to Valam, they were to be found in the mountains that were the border between east and west, and it was their true home. They had come at Teren's bidding and because they believed it was time to let their presence be known.

Chapter Fourteen

Noman, Xith, and the others departed Zashchita just as the darkness of night waned. Shchander discussed the news he and his men had learned while at the inn. Noman was very pleased to note that word of the princess' disappearance was heard on no one's lips. Xith was also pleased; however, Y'sat's words still weighed heavily on his conscious, as he assumed they did on Noman, but Noman carried them better. Xith considered it good fortune, though, that most of the news was pleasant.

The next two days passed relatively slowly as they forgot the enchantment of the city. The dark specters that seemed to be with them before they had reached Zashchita returned and it was with heavy hearts that Noman and Xith kept on. Their thoughts often went to Ayrian and to Vilmos—the two that seemed to be lost to them—and to Adrina—the one who they seemed to be losing.

They held to the main roads through brief stretches of open prairie, yet mostly they moved through thick, lush forest greens. Growth in this area was very different from the heavy pine, tall oak, ash, elm and even a few cedars and walnut. An abundant mixture grew in the old forest, but the great forest now lay far to their west. Here the trees tended to be thick groves. Those they rode through now were beautiful, deep, and green, and the pungent smell of pine assaulted their nostrils. Ahead lay a large stand of thick, dark-wood trees that stretched out far beyond their view, which was apparent only because of the high, fir-covered hills they rode along now. Each time they mounted a new hill, a different piece of the land ahead was revealed to them as they peered out through the branches.

Adrina was bored as she sat in the carriage with the sun lightly playing across her face. She rubbed the mark glumly; she could feel life within very often now. She stared openly at the one who sat directly across from her, hoping her eyes would stir his tongue although it had not yet in many hours of riding.

When they entered the thick, dark wood, it became quickly apparent to Adrina, for the sun vanished. She did not have the advantage of looking out over the horizon to see what lay ahead. She moved close to the wall of the carriage, hugging it close, feeling comfort in its presence beside her.

"Do you ever speak?" questioned Adrina, driving away the darkness she perceived with her words. "Do you have a name?" she further asked before a response could be rendered. "Are you always this tight-lipped?" queried Adrina.

"Seldom, and yes on both accounts, Princess Adrina."

"What is it?"

"What is what?"

"Your name?"

"Shalimar," quietly whispered the man, as if his name were an evil thing.

"That is a nice name," returned Adrina, attempting to stir his tongue.

Shalimar's only response was a slight smile, which was quick to fade as his eyes resumed their far-away stare. He longed to be elsewhere although he was also happy to be right here. His feelings were very mixed.

Afternoon shadows soon came; and shortly afterward, night fell around them. They made camp not far from the road, far enough so they were out of sight but close enough so it would be easy to leave if the need arose. The coach was their primary concern; it could not travel over rough terrain and needed a clear path. It also cast a large shadow, one passers-by might see if they looked closely.

Another day arrived and went, then two more passed. The country they were in was very different from that which they were accustomed to, but the changes were very subtle. The land had a feel of wildness to it, and a sense that most of it laid untouched by the hands of man. The road narrowed to a wide path, but tracks were deep along it although they had met no one since they had departed Zashchita, a fact that did not seem significant to them.

Xith was quietly brooding; he and Noman had just had a very lengthy argument, which Xith felt that he had lost. After thinking about it, he decided he would not let the questions sit. He clipped his mount and raced up alongside Noman. "I still do not like it. I tell you, I feel an absence. At least let me try, just a little test, a mere spark."

"Xith, I do not think it is wise; perhaps we are free of any who would follow, but afterwards, who would know?"

"Do you not believe the words of Y'sat?"

"Yes, I do, but we must wait."

Xith couldn't help the smile that lit his lips and cheeks. He liked to see the fire revive in Noman's eyes. He turned to respond, but as he did the happiness left his face and the group came to a sudden halt. Amir's sword danced in his hands as he reined in his mount alongside Noman.

"The forest has eyes," called out Amir.

"Yes, I know," said Noman, turning to smile at Xith. "Put away your weapon. They will do us no harm this day."

Without question, Amir lowered his sword and sheathed it. He then spurred his mount towards Nijal, to the forward watch. Shchander and a few of his men still claimed the rear watch, and they trotted along at a good pace behind the coach. Adrina still sat discontented in the carriage with the tightlipped Shalimar to watch over her. Although she was thankful that the face remained the same before her, she wished Shalimar would say something more than a morning and nightly greeting, which was nothing more than courteous speech.

Night found them as their path came to a small tributary of the great river, the Krasnyj, which was flowing very well in these eastern lands that they rode through. Morning came, bright and cheerful, with late afternoon catching them looping down a gently sloping hill into a vast, high-rimmed vale with a lake sweeping across most of its midsection. The last sounds of birds and day creatures left them as night arrived, and the sounds of night appeared in their place with the gentle croaking of frogs, the song of crickets, and a soft northerly wind.

Xith cast off the dark shadows that had hung over him for days, and all found time to bathe in the lake before retiring under the starlit sky. Noman knew the lake and the surrounding valley; it was a near halfway point on their journey and a pleasant place to relax and forget the worries of travel and all else that lay behind for a time. He also recalled a name for it, though he would not say if someone had asked him. He preferred the ways of old, when naught had name except that given to it by the Mother. A tree was a tree and a valley was a valley. He remembered a people of long ago, which he knew were now scattered far across the seas; and staring out over the gray waters before him, he wondered how they fared. He did not know what suddenly brought on the peculiar thoughts, but they came; perhaps it was the stranger that he had touched in Adrina's mind some time ago, or perhaps a distant thought had triggered his recollection.

It was late morning before they could draw themselves away from the pleasant shore, find the strength to move around it to the far side, and take the road up and out of the valley. Laughter had found and lightened many a heavy heart. Adrina had finally been able to carry on a conversation with someone other than herself. She had felt that everyone had been shunning her as if they feared her or she had a disease. Now she was happy, and a smile touched her lips and brightened her cheeks.

As they mounted the steep hills, they looked back over their shoulders down into the pleasant lake; only Noman searched beyond to the edges of the forest, seeking something that was not there. The eagerness of morning was quick to fade as a light drizzle found them late in the day, continuing until the night. A deep chill loomed in the air of the camp that night, and very skilled hands worked long and hard to build a fire to warm cold bodies.

The wet weather stayed with them for three more days, rutting the roads and slowing their movement to a crawl. They again found themselves amidst the green and brown of forests; in fact, this had been true since they completed their uphill ascent of several days ago. Here the land was mostly flat although it held a slight downhill slope much of the time. The air seemed to be growing colder each day as the weather grew more and more foul. The sight of snow would not have surprised them.

Now they lunched in a small clearing just off the road, stopping to wait out a hard downpour and using the time to rest weary animals and to bring nourishment to their own tired souls. Long into the afternoon they waited for the storm to pass or let up from its long torment, but it did not. So here they were forced to make their camp for the night. Neither spark from skilled hands nor flint rock brought fire to the wet wood they gathered, and still fearing their use of magic, this night passed by cold and wet, without the benefits of a fire.

Scattered shouts in the night roused the sentry, and soon everyone was awake or mostly awake, returning to sleep only when weapons were close at hand and the shadows in the woods had long since passed. Amir was last on watch and first to greet the early rays of a dawning day, a day that he sensed would be clear and cloudless. He was also the first to discover that Adrina was missing.

Chapter Fifteen

Clouds moving across the night sky brought shadows, dark and odd to the land. Calyin and Midori followed Lord Serant and Geoffrey. Captain Brodst kept to the rear. They used the darkness as their blanket, pulling it with them, carrying it along beside and around them, pausing momentarily when it slipped back from on top of them, and moving again when it returned. Lord Serant moved his feet with great determination and much perseverance. He wondered at the strength of those with him; he had heard no complaints since they had made their escape from Imtal even when his own body felt like a weight pulling him into the ground.

On the backside of a low, sloping hill, amidst a small stand of tightly packed oak, they stopped for what remained of the night. They could go no farther. It was here that Calyin finally broke into tears, great heavy sobs that were muffled within her lord husband's strong embrace. "Oh Edwar," she whispered to him. "So many lost and for what?"

Lord Edwar Serant stood firm. He moved Midori and the others back with his eyes as he put Calyin at arm's length. "If there are any who must hold strong, it is us," he told her. "We must hold strong and remain true to each other and Great Kingdom. There will be a time for retribution."

Calyin sucked at the air and forced her mind to calm. She was an Alder and the strength of her family ran in her veins. For a fleeting moment her eyes turned accusingly to her sister. The unspoken words that passed between the two were clear to each. Calyin at first blamed the other and then forgave. Midori, who had once considered herself an Alder but was no more, accepted her share of blame but patently refused forgiveness. If there was to be forgiveness, it would come from the Mother.

In two-hour shifts, they switched the watch; though tired and weary of body and mind, none slept soundly, and morning found them in much the same state they had been the night before— drained. Travel by day was a poor choice but a necessity. They were still in the kingdom and to their knowledge only Imtal had fallen, so they pressed on cautiously.

The bright warmth of the sun brought no cheer. In the distance in the east, storm clouds loomed, as if they were a sign, and towards the east they continued. For a time that morning, they followed a shallow stream that afforded them water cool and soothing until mid-day, for which they were very thankful for they had no water skins with them. The water sustained their empty bellies, yet it did not satisfy the rumblings of hunger within.

Lord Serant promised that Kauj lay just ahead, and if they maintained a good pace, taking adequate breaks; they would reach it late in the evening. The others well knew where the city of Kauj lay, but with Serant's words the promise became real to them, and they strove for it. They stayed well away from the road, following the gullies and ditches in and around the hill country they walked through.

Midori perceived a hint of the Mother with her this day, for which she was very thankful. She had been so empty without another presence in her consciousness. Late in the afternoon, she dared to touch the will of the land with hers, and was pleased when it flowed back to her. The domain of the Mother was hers again, and she was ecstatic. Guidance flowed to her mind as if she had regained her sight although she still perceived an absence around her.

As they stopped just before dusk to insure that they were not off course, a call came to her crisply from the wood a short distance away. It bade her to hurry to its confines until the darkness approached. Midori quickly led her companions to the shadows of the wood and they followed her unquestioningly.

They had no more than reached the trees and found cover when they heard the clatter of hooves. They did not move again until long after the silence returned. From then on, they moved even farther away from the road. Movement this night became difficult as the stars of the previous night were completely blocked by clouded skies. Later, the road was very difficult to find in the darkness.

A distant sound of music coming from the north reached their ears. Puzzled, they continued swiftly, pausing only briefly. Those that wore hooded cloaks, pulled them close around themselves, and those that didn't raised their collars high. The sight of buildings in the distance brought relief to their heavy hearts.

Unfortunately, Kauj only had a single inn. Tiny as it was, they still hoped to take a brief respite before they continued on their way. With luck, they would not have to remain the entire night, and they would hopefully be able to purchase horses. Their minds were consumed with thoughts of food and warmth.

Geoffrey went alone into Kauj while the others waited at a safe distance. He visited the inn first; then he sought out the stables. The inn was very quiet. He saw only two customers, solemnly sipping their draught, and the innkeeper. He stepped just into the doorway but did not inquire about rooms. He went back to the street.

He knew of two stables in Kauj, or at least there used to be two stables. He walked to the nearest one, which appeared to be in business although it was secured for the night, as he had thought it would be at this hour. Upon cursory inspection, he counted several horses in the corral to the rear, but they appeared to be mostly nags. He could not see within the stable stalls, but any horse was better than walking, so he was not completely discouraged.

Afterward he rejoined the others and led the way to the inn. Once inside, they were quick to inquire about rooms. The innkeeper had three empty but one was already promised. They would have to share the two, which suited them; they would have taken only one. They also ordered food to be brought to their rooms, but the innkeeper could only promise them gruel and hard bread at this hour. They did not refuse this either.

They were quick to retire to their rooms but not before Lord

Serant and Captain Brodst eyed the two who sat in the far corner drinking. Something about them caught their interest. Cautiously, the captain queried about the two, pretending to have an interest in peddling his wares to them. The innkeeper told him that he hadn't seen the two before and that they were not very friendly, so he recommended staying clear of them. Captain Brodst smiled and said thanks and then went upstairs.

The gruel, which they would normally have considered tasteless, was very welcome and satisfying. After eating their fill and washing up, they slept, and it was morning before any of them awoke. Calyin was the first to awaken, and startled by how high the sun was, woke the others.

All took turns cursing themselves for their error, but it could not be denied that the sleep had done them good. As long as they were already here past morning, they would eat and gather provisions for the journey ahead. Brodst was the one chosen to venture downstairs, which he did.

The inn was fairly busy this morning, mostly with travelers stopping only for a quick meal as they passed through, or so it appeared. The captain did not delay in making arrangements for supplies and horses and soon returned to where the others waited, gathered all in one room. Captain Brodst admitted that he did not like the feel of the inn this morning; he perceived something amiss though he knew not what.

The rattle of trays startled them as several were placed on the hall floor. Directly afterwards came a knock on the door, a soft rapping.

Captain Brodst answered the door, pulling it open only

partially. He recognized the servant as the one from last night, and sighed, accepting the food graciously. Sometime later, the servant returned to retrieve the trays and dishes. He also informed the captain that the foodstuffs he had wanted were ready, and that he had sent a message to the stable master. Captain Brodst thanked the boy and gave him a small coin as a token of thanks.

"What do we do now?" asked Calyin of Serant. "Do you still think it is safe to journey to Solntse this day?"

"If that is still our course, I say yes."

"If?" asked Geoffrey. "I thought we were set."

"I am not so sure now. I think—I'm not sure what I think, but I sense something."

"Yes, the Mother speaks to me this morning from afar; this does not bode well. I also think a change of course would be better."

"I would still rather be in Imtal; at least there I would know the specters."

"A change of words, I believe, is in order. It is not good to mention things of darkness, lest they come."

"I am sorry, Sister. I regress," the captain spoke the words with a grin on his face, as he stared at Midori, who stared back at him with an equally knowing smile.

"If we change our course, what of the warning? Have you pondered the meaning of the things they said to us?" spoke Calyin, her eyes mostly falling on Midori, who understood best of all, she thought.

"The words were not meant to confuse us, as was already

said, but merely to make us think, to make us give deep consideration to our path, and yes to give us a direction to begin and end in. The in-between, I think, is mostly up to us."

"Let's delay no further. I want to put a great distance between us and Kauj."

"Lord Serant is right; we should be off."

Geoffrey went to collect and pay for the horses, which he purchased without trouble, while Captain Brodst saw to their provisions and Serant retrieved some water skins and other miscellaneous items from a nearby merchant. Midori and Calyin remained at the inn, passing the time by talking as only two sisters do. Thoughts of Adrina and Andrew carried over into their conversation; they missed them both.

Fortunately, the nags they rode upon proved to have good stamina; and by late afternoon, the shadows they perceived in Kauj seemed to be far behind them. The sense of nature surrounding them put Midori at ease. As they rode, she turned her thoughts inward for a time of reflection. She was the first of the Mother, yet she observed certain reservations she knew others before her had not. Her thoughts flowed to a figure. The face of an old man came before her and she wondered how he fared. He had not returned as he said he would, and she needed his support, his guidance.

She thought about time and wondered where she would be during the vernal equinox, when the time of her calling came. She did not know whom she would choose, but surely, as the first, she must choose. She thought about the other priestesses at sanctuary, and how they fared without her guidance. They knew that the first, second and third were gone, and perhaps, she thought, they may be lost. As she dwelled on this, she knew this to be false. Her mouth fell agape and now she understood the emptiness. They had crossed the rights and transcended without her. "Why, Mother?" cried Midori in her thoughts. "Why did you sanction this?"

"Midori?" called Brodst. "Are you all right? You look so pale."

"Yes—yes, I am fine," softly responded Midori, sadness evident in her voice. "Fine, fine, fine," laughed Midori, sarcastically. She bit her lip and thus stopped further words from issuing from her mouth. She pulled her hood tight about her face and withdrew into its recesses and cried heavy mournful sobs.

Chapter Sixteen

The words of the mountaineers were odd to Valam's ears; somehow, they were in the same tongue as Seth yet different. He was glad they were quick to adapt to his own language, which greatly enhanced their ability to communicate. He decided that they were a strong bunch, and the power was not only in their hands and minds, but also in their hearts. They were free spirits. He also found that they were quick to sudden anger, and quick to turn from it and laugh. They played with emotions sending it as the most prevalent item in all their thoughts, using it to their own advantage.

Their skin and eyes were a deep, burnt tan in contrast to Seth's paler skin. The plains had been harsh on them, and these were the first of Seth's kind. Valam wondered whether the signs of wear and tear on their features were the result of great age or simply evidence of the harshness of their lives on the plains. Ekharn was their leader although they claimed to have no leader. They counted all of their kind as equals.

A small group gathered in the center of the camp, preparing to depart. This day they would journey back to the mountains with Teren as their guide. With hesitation, Father Jacob gave his blessing for Prince Valam to accompany the party as Ekharn wished and with a very heavy heart he watched the band leave the confines of the camp. He hoped Valam would never leave his sight again, and he was torn with lament as if he was losing what he had only recently found.

Valam smiled courteously in response to Yulorien's words floating through his mind, but momentarily he cast his attentions back to Jacob, whose countenance spoke many things. It wasn't until much, much later, as they plodded through the rocky coastline north, that he realized what was said to him. He repeated the words in his thoughts, "No, my friend, the Queen-Mother holds no dominion over the mountain folk, although we do count her blessings."

The journey along the coast to Ekharn's camp took only one full day. This time of year often found them encamped on steep bluffs jutting out into the sea, the mountains rising high behind them, and in front of them the plains. As they mounted the bluff, Valam caught sight of a white snowcap on the mountains as far as he could see. The places he was led into seemed at first gloomy and foreboding, but soon they were streaming with light and cheer.

Passageways that began with great canyons became narrower and shallower, tunnels that were made by skilled hands with chisel and hammer. They wove together a series of interconnecting rooms, halls, dwellings and much more that were all natural and would have been otherwise inaccessible. Valam felt empty without Evgej, Seth, and the others who had been his constant companions for a very long time. They had been forbidden to accompany the mountaineers although exception had been made in the case of Mikhal and Danyel' and the two were in the party today.

The three and Teren now sat in an enormous hollow awaiting Ekharn's return. Yulorien sat with them although he did not speak. Valam regarded the rock-hewn benches they were seated upon, set in a semi-circle around the chamber. In the center of the room an earthen hearth spewed warmth, its smoke drifting into an unseen chimney.

A lengthy hour later, Ekharn returned, and as he did Yulorien stood and bowed his head. As a polite gesture, Valam did the same and the others except Teren, who did not move, followed his lead. Behind Ekharn walked a woman in a white flowing gown. Once she was seated, Yulorien raised his head, and after momentarily regarding her, he took his place.

"You need not pay homage to me," whispered a voice, powerful, yet feminine, casting with it an expression of warmth and also a feeling of welcome. "I have no persuasion over you or any of your kind, though I am the Mother of my people."

"The Queen-Mother," flashed through Valam's thoughts before he considered that his mind was open.

"I am no queen, I have no kingdom nor any domain, unless you count the lands you place your feet upon now, but they are not mine to offer, even to myself."

"I am sorry," said Valam. "I did not mean to—"

"There is no need for apology; no offense was taken or given. I brought you here so I could speak openly with you without fear of reprisal. There are those who would not look favorably upon my presence, and there are those who do not know that I exist. I wish it to be kept so at least for now. Do you know that the Mother of the Eastern Reaches attempted to send your people away before your arrival?"

Valam's eyes and thoughts gave evidence of the direction he thought the conversation flowed. Teren jumped to his feet almost immediately. "I am no traitor to my people, Prince Valam, of this I assure you."

"Please, Brother Teren, seat yourself. He will see the truth of it; give him time. You are no traitor." Her words flowed, mixed with truth and understanding to all present. A suppressed message of "wait, and you will see," was also sent with it simultaneously. "I want you to know the facts; this is why I have brought you here. You are being played like an errant pawn. The fool is one step away from obtaining the swordmasterless king."

"King?"

"Do you not think that I know? I see all, but little do I question until it is time. Once there were two queens and two kings in the lands beyond the seas, the lands that now lie in desolation, so the balance was held in check, but no more. We are here, and yours are there. Valam, a prince, an heir, a king, a pauper."

"Do you mock me?"

"No, I praise you. Do you not understand? Regard what I have said, and in time you will come to know."

"I am at a loss," said Valam.

"You are at no loss and understand me well. The words I have spoken are not beyond your minds, but beyond your ears.

You hear but do not listen."

Valam returned to the first words spoken to him and asked, "Why would the Queen-Mother send away those she needs."

"You know the answer. She told you herself. Think!"

A flood of remembrance came upon Valam and carried him away. The world about him became gray and shadowy, and if Teren had not protected his head from the stone, he would have slammed against it when he collapsed forward. He saw the paths in his thoughts, a vision that played out two-fold for him, overwhelming him and sending his body into shock as the vision came to the end, as he saw his life come to an end. Now he understood Tsandra's words, but it was too late; the moment had passed.

As light returned to his eyes, Valam was unsure how long he had been lost or if he had been lost at all. He opened his eyes, and he was still seated where he had been; Teren, Mikhal, Danyel', and the others were all still there. "How long have I been gone?"

"The length is not the key, it is the knowledge. Now, do you understand?"

"Yes, I remember, but why did I forget, and how did I—I was dead."

"You were and you weren't. As is this, that was but a crossing, a possibility that is now passed, but now you have the answers, and what will you do with them?"

"I, I—do not know."

"I will give you time. In your heart, you will know what to do, and you will do it, but heed this. That which you think is occurring usually is not, and that which you do not expect probably is. Do not regard her falsely, for she does not hold you thus. She did only what she considered just, and perhaps it was. Now that you have seen the many lines, you know what your fate would have been at each turning. But now you are beyond the turnings, and I can show you no more."

"I saw myself die more than once. How can this be?"

"As I have stated, this was your past. Yes, you would have perished if you had stayed in the kingdom, and—"

"Then what I saw is real."

"Perhaps, but possibly it is only what could have been if you had been there. I cannot say, but you must consider it in your heart of hearts and act accordingly."

"And the second time?"

"Yes, another possibility, but do not dwell thus on the past. Move forward and decide; this is why we have returned. Why I have given you counsel. You must know all paths and decide for yourself which to take."

"Why do you help me? And why, Teren, did you allow me to come here? I still do not understand."

Teren paused and let the other speak first. "I help you because I must; there is no other reason."

"You must?"

"Prince Valam, I also do what I feel is right and just for my people."

"It is all right, Brother Teren, you do not need to justify yourself in his eyes; he does understand if he will only consider. I wish not to say more, but I will add this: a gift is not always free;

it often has its costs, and now the balance is brought back in check."

Valam began to speak, but he was cut short and bade to be silent. "'Why are Danyel' and Mikhal here, you think. Consider your own thoughts. Your path is with them, not the others. Alas, I have said too much; you must go."

"Go?"

"Yes, but only from this chamber. Return with all haste to Leklorall and ask of the queen your questions. Ask her of the sword as well. Awaken now and remember." Her last words carried much more than simple litany. As with everything she had said to him, mingled with it were a mixture a feelings and deep emotion that would take Valam some time to sort out if he could do it at all.

Valam watched her as she walked away, and just before she entered an adjacent corridor to disappear from sight, she glanced back at him and said again stronger and with more urgency, "Awaken now and remember."

Chapter Seventeen

Adrina was missing. The camp spun with excited activity. Shchander and his men were sent to search the woods in the immediate vicinity while Nijal and Amir set to finding Adrina's tracks. Noman and Xith were quick to collapse into sudden but friendly argument. They didn't discover until much later that one of Shchander's men was also missing.

By afternoon, troubled eyes stared desperately to Xith and Noman who were still arguing. Xith soon turned to Shchander with many questions, to which Shchander could respond honestly. Shalimar was a man to be trusted, and he held no ill in his heart. Xith turned to Nijal, regarding his nervousness and asked, "Did she say anything to you, anything at all that you counted odd?"

Nijal was slow to speak, but he did. "That night, I had an odd—no, it was nothing."

"Speak, man," said Noman commanding Nijal to bring words to his lips. "All things have significance."

"The night Adrina woke screaming, when I coaxed her to return to the carriage. I watched her. I saw her eyes as she lay there. She was afraid, very afraid. For hours I kept watch, hoping she would drift off to sleep, but she never did. I am not sure, but sometime during the time I was there I had a dream. I may have closed my eyes for five minutes or for several hours, I am not sure. When I awoke, her eyes were upon me as if she knew the dream I dreamt. She asked me again if we could go outside, and this time I did so without hesitation."

"The dream, what was it?" asked Xith intrigued.

"A voice," replied Nijal.

"A voice?"

As Nijal began, his voice quivered and his hands twitched nervously. "After that, I did not want to be near her. It was a very strange thing. It is my fault. I should have been with her, not Shalimar."

"Nijal, stop babbling. Go back to the dream. Tell me about the voice."

"The voice?"

"Yes, the voice, tell me about it. Nothing can hurt you. Close your eyes and tell us about the dream and the voice."

Nijal closed his eyes, and all became silent around him as the others waited for him to speak. Nijal still was hesitant; he thought it best to let his dream be lost. "I was surrounded by darkness, so much darkness, and he was there. He came out of the darkness, which seemed to follow him, and after a time, I could see, as if my eyes focused. Black flames licked the air, streaming from dark coffers. He was seated on an ebony throne. He bade Adrina to give him the child, but she would not—" Nijal's voice faded off, and he broke down into sudden sobs.

Xith looked to Noman, who returned his concern. "Nijal,

listen closely, who are they that Adrina spoke of?"

"The shadows, they spoke to her—and the dragons, they spoke to her."

"When?" demanded Noman, looming over Nijal.

Nijal cowered down to his knees, "Once out of the blackness, they asked her to follow them."

"And you did not tell us? What were you thinking, Nijal, son of Geoffrey?" yelled Shchander angrily, cursing Nijal the only way he knew how.

"Wait, do not be harsh with him. I can see it on his face; he only now remembers. He did not know himself until he spoke the words. Is that not so?" stated Noman, his tone now very kind and understanding.

"Yes," replied Nijal honestly. He said nothing of Tnavres, the tiny dragon Adrina harbored, though later he would be unable to explain what held his tongue.

Noman began to speak again, but he stopped, and then turned, his eyes wild with surprise and relief. "Amir, Shalimar—Adrina?"

"I found them," said Amir, "and you won't believe this, only about a half hour walk from here. Gathering flowers, the truth be known."

"White flowers growing along a peaceful stream; it was so serene there," said Adrina.

"Flowers?" demanded Xith, losing his temper briefly.

"Yes, beautiful white flowers. I picked some for you," said Adrina, offering Xith a bouquet, and as he accepted them, staring into her eyes of pure innocence, he forgave her and said nothing further on the subject. Noman started to object, but as she handed him a grouping of flowers, he held back, only chastising softly, telling her never to go off alone again, to which she responded that she hadn't gone off alone.

All thoughts of dark shadows were cast aside, and soon they were moving rapidly along the trail, trying to make up some of the lost time. Only one significant change had occurred, and it was that now only Amir and Nijal would ride with Adrina and keep watch over her. No one chastised Shalimar, as he had already punished himself and repented wholly for his mistake, which had been an honest one.

Noman saw Adrina in a new light from then on. She had the gift of persuasion, there could be no doubt. She knew how to get what she wanted. Shalimar was no fool. He had been led astray and by what Noman suspected could only be the guiles of the Voice—a thing that would be most troubling if it were true.

Chapter Eighteen

Gray skies hovered overhead as night came, and the group stopped. Midori counted her blessings, for they had made good progress this day, and it had passed without incident. She cheered up but not until long after she lay down to sleep and well after her shift at watch. Sleep finally came to her just as she considered the possibility that maybe, just maybe, she was at a crossing, a time when there could be two who were first to the Mother. She recalled despondently the fact that not long ago she had been only the fourth to the Mother; and even with Jasmine and Catrin's demise there was another who by all accounts should have progressed to the highest position before her.

It was Calyin who awoke Midori some hours later by shaking her softly. Calyin had held the final watch and she awoke her sister before waking the others. "We must talk," Calyin said quietly, pointing to a place away from the others.

Midori nodded and followed Calyin into the darkness.

"The men are divided," Calyin whispered when they were a safe distance away from the camp. "My lord husband wishes to escape to the north. Geoffrey and the captain wish to rouse the garrisons of High Road and Solntse, then return to Imtal. They say Great Kingdom has not fallen, that only Imtal has fallen.

What does the Mother tell you?"

Midori wanted to tell Calyin that the Mother told her she was not the true first and that the Mother was so distant from her that it seemed she was alone. Those things were not exactly the truth, however, and she held her tongue saying instead what was safest. "Imtal has fallen, the Kingdom lives on."

"What of the Great Houses? What of the garrisons? Can you sense anything?"

"She senses," said Lord Serant approaching out of the darkness, "the great change is upon us."

"My lord husband," Calyin said formerly turning to face Edwar Serant.

"You speak now behind my back?" he asked her.

Calyin lowered her eyes momentarily, then looked directly at him. "She is my sister. We are Alders, despite what she thinks. We do not run and hide."

Lord Serant spat openly. "You think I run willingly? You are my wife. You who should know me better than any."

"My lord husband, I never met to imply cowardice. I seek only answers. The Delinna I once knew was strong and resolute. Even in the face of our father, she stood to her convictions."

Lord Serant beaded his eyes and said louder than the previous whispers, "Are you saying I lack conviction?"

Midori thrust herself between the two. "I am right here," she said. "Don't speak of me as if I am lost. I made my choices and I have no regrets."

Calyin whirled around to face Midori. "Shall we then get it all out in the open?" Her voice was full of venom as she spoke. "I hated you for what you did. I hated you for your choices. But I respected you for your choices as well. You had only to speak his name and father would have had him swinging from the rope. It would have satisfied all, would it not have?"

"No," said Midori emphatically, tears in her eyes. "It would not have satisfied anything. Don't you see that it was about power? He couldn't have cared less about honor and the word bond of our father."

"He?" cut in Lord Serant.

The strong words had by now roused Geoffrey Solntse and Captain Ansh Brodst. Both were standing not far off. "They speak of King Jarom," said Captain Brodst knowingly.

"Stay out of this," said Midori and Calyin at the same time. Calyin added, "You've done quite enough already."

"Just what's that supposed to mean?" asked Midori. "Ansh could no more have held back than I could have."

Afraid the two sisters were about to come to blows, Lord Serant gripped Calyin's wrists. "We must return to the road."

Calyin held firm. "No, not until we've said what must be said."

"Agreed," Midori said, returning her sister's glare.

"Say it," demanded Calyin. "Say that father was wrong. Say that you were wrong. Say that you are an Alder by blood and by blood you hold."

"I will say no such thing, Calyin. You will never know how hard it was for me to walk away. To leave Imtal. To leave all that I knew. To leave him. You may think the Priestesses of the Mother are beyond the affairs of the Kingdoms and hold true to none, but this is not so. Our duty, our first duty, is to the peoples of Ruin Mist. I did what I must because the Mother showed me the paths. Marrying Jarom Tyr'anth would have only hastened the path of destruction. Surely you know this—you must know this."

Calyin was trembling. Serant released his grip on her wrists and embraced her. "Enough," he said. "You are sisters by blood, and by blood you hold. I can see it if you do not. We must return to the road now or all will be lost."

Like thieves in the night, they began anew. Lord Serant assumed the lead and Geoffrey took the rear. Captain Brodst rode beside Midori and Calyin. Several hours of veiled sky remained before dawn and they were going to put this time to good use. Until just before first light, they maintained the road, and shortly afterwards they moved far to its outskirts.

The land had gentle, gradual slopes going downhill. In the distance they could now see the ridges that marked the Borderlands, and beyond them the snow-capped mountains of the north. Geoffrey knew this region the best as it was within the area patrolled by his fellows. In his youth, he had been on many patrols in this area himself. The closest garrison of the kingdom lay where the borders of the Barrens, the Borderlands, and the Great Kingdom met; and now they had just moved beyond its grasp.

They still thought it queer that they should attempt to avoid the very ones who should by all means be their confederates, but they would still follow caution and hope it was folly when they reached Solntse. As afternoon came upon them, they saw several patrols pass along the road at a distance, and an ever-increasing amount of traffic. This was not odd at all. They saw groups of wagons, riders, and even people on foot. Sometimes the passersby traveled in mixed groups but always they had some sort of armed company with them, usually an escort of two to three men heavily equipped, who probably required higher fees than would the rogues who could have found them.

An attack by outlaws was now Lord Serant's primary concern also, for they had not much to offer in the way of monetary gain. They stayed close together with eyes constantly on guard and hands always at the ready. Serant gave heavy consideration to moving beyond the kingdom borders and into the borderlands. He didn't believe all the tales he had heard about the place; but if so many believed them, it would surely be a good place to be. The rain that had held off in previous days found them at first morning light as a drizzle but it quickly turned into a downpour. They sought cover or, possibly, to outrun it. Unbeknownst to them as they raced to escape the storm, their course turned northerly; and before they knew it, the land had turned to rock and crag. However, they did not stop, nor did they heed their own instincts.

Lightning crackled in the air around them, sending sparks of energy through the air, and growing ever nearer. Their steeds turned of their own accord as the brilliant bolts struck within a few feet of horse and rider, and all the riders could do was to hold on and pray they could maintain their mounts. The sound of thunder suddenly swallowed all sound, and a split second later a flash lit the sky to their immediate left. Midori fell on the hard rock as her horse reared.

As she fell to the ground, she rolled away from the horse's feet, which were seeking unintentionally to stomp her life away. Both Lord Serant and Captain Brodst saw her fall, but only the captain could turn his mount around to offer her a quick hand. The reins stung as they bit into his hand, but he did not release his right grip. He grasped her arm at the elbow and was able to pull her to safety.

Midori rubbed the sore spot on her head only for a moment before she locked both arms around Brodst's waist. She wasn't going to fall again if she could help it. She searched for her horse, but it was now long gone, lost among the ridges and the many turns in the path. A spot of white caught her eye; it almost looked as if a clear area lay in front of them, but she wasn't quite sure.

Suddenly, they broke past the clouds, the rain stopped, the lightning receded, and the setting sun filled their field of vision. Captain Brodst reined his horse to a sudden halt. Directly in front of him, the path fell away into a very steep downward slope. As he gazed, he saw that they were on the very edge of an enormous valley—more a ravine than a valley. As he looked, he changed his mind. It was definitely a canyon, narrow and deep, winding like a great serpent through the rock.

"Downward—" whispered Midori.

Geoffrey didn't like the looks of the place; his choice was to wait until the storms passed and turn back toward Solntse. "We must go to the garrison; only then will we know."

Captain Brodst had heard Midori's faint murmur. She had whispered almost directly into his ear. He gave weight to both Geoffrey's and Midori's words. "I say we follow Geoffrey to

Solntse," stated Brodst.

"I say," started Serant, "that we continue along our current path and see where it takes us."

Calyin was the only one who had not spoken her mind, and the other four turned toward her to hear her opinion. She wasn't as quick to make a judgment as the others and she returned Midori's wry look to her. Midori thanked Captain Brodst and dismounted.

"I believe we should continue; there is much at hand that we do not understand, and it is best to follow when led, to see where the path takes us."

"Three to two," spoke Geoffrey sadly. He shrugged his shoulders, shedding the sense of foreboding he perceived, and urged his mount onward at a cautious pace. After Midori mounted behind Calyin, the rest followed his lead; and as they journeyed down into the depths of the canyon, the darkness of night seemed to come immediately over them or at least its shadows did. The sky overhead was still a washed-out blue.

The descent was extremely drawn-out since they had to follow a staggered path crisscrossing the wall of the canyon many times. By the time they found the canyon floor, it was too dark to continue. The rush of water led them on for a time until they came to the edge of a river, where they made camp. They did manage to find enough scrub brush in the immediate area to get a blazing fire burning, giving no heed to precaution.

Lord Serant clapped a hand to Geoffrey's back in response to his far-off stare during their evening meal. "It isn't that bad, my friend. Soon you will be home with nothing but time on your hands, and all this will be far behind you, behind all of us."

"I hope so," responded Geoffrey weakly, "I hope so."

The captain, who had wandered off in search of more wood, returned. His eyes were almost as distant as Geoffrey's as he sat next to Serant. He looked to Midori and Calyin who quietly watched the flames, and then to Geoffrey and Serant. "Do you really think so?" asked Brodst.

"It is the desire of my heart, yes."

"Lord Serant, I mean no disrespect when I say, this—I have been thinking very carefully—"

"Don't—" whispered Midori.

"I must go to Solntse. We are only a full day's ride away—we cannot turn away. What of the garrison troops there in full company? Tomorrow, I will go alone if need be, but to Solntse, I will go."

Captain Brodst spoke the words that had been on the tip of Geoffrey's tongue, and Geoffrey was quick to add his opinion, which was to go to Solntse. "We'll take the capital back by force. We'll round the garrisons from the whole of the kingdom! And we'll march on Imtal and drive Jarom back to his lands as we would a mad dog!" Two pairs of eyes fell to Lord Serant, and wondered why he held his thoughts in check, and why he would continue along this path, which was completely against his nature.

"Do not say your thoughts!" announced Serant. "Or I'll cut out your tongues myself. I thought we gave this great consideration before we began this journey. Our path is fated—" As Lord Serant continued to speak at length, Geoffrey understood Lord Serant's reasoning even though the captain did not, for he understood the superstitious nature of those of the Territories and the captain did not. Honor took second place to beliefs, which were very strongly based. Geoffrey also saw the hatred Lord Serant held for Midori, not because he disliked her personally but because she had the power to hold his fears over him and show them to him.

The night was calm with the gentle sound of the river lulling their thoughts for a time. Lord Serant opted for the first watch, and he remained on guard all through the night, waking no one to replace him. The stars appeared so very far off as he stared at them; they did not bring answers to his questions, for he did not seek the answers. The blackness of night slowly dissipated replaced by morning light, but no sun.

Geoffrey and Captain Brodst parted from the others as morning came; the three who sat around the fire watched them retreat without saying a word. Lord Serant, Calyin and Midori would continue on their own. The canyon floor proved to be very rough and strewn with boulders, making it extremely difficult to traverse. With only two horses to bear the burden of three, they would walk this day.

Their thoughts were with the two who went to Solntse. They did not fear for their own safety. Three could survive as easily as could five and three could possibly remain more invisible than five. Before, they would have retreated from any force and that had not changed. A fight was not what they sought, so they would not confront a hostile force. They continued on through the rains and sleet, downward, inward, outward, upward, wherever their feet led them.

Chapter Nineteen

"Valam? Valam?" asked Jacob. "I am finished." Jacob nudged Valam a second time with no response. He quickly began to speak again, "I am sorry, gentlemen, for taking up so much of your time, but now I conclude and give you to Prince Valam."

"Valam? Valam?" said Jacob, louder than he wished. He smiled graciously and then apologized. He shook Valam, who was slow to open his eyes. "My prince, I am most sorry. Perhaps we should delay this meeting until tomorrow."

Valam opened his eyes, blinked once, then blinked again. "Captain Mikhal?" asked Valam.

"He has not yet arrived, I am sorry."

Valam sat up straight and looked around the tent. His eyes opened wide. "Ekharn? Where did Ekharn go?"

Sensing something was wrong, Father Jacob dismissed all present saying, "Let us adjourn until this evening, or better still, tomorrow morning. I apologize again most graciously."

Valam stood, excused himself, and walked out, but just before the entry, he turned back to look at those seated around the table, and he smiled and said, "Eran, brother of Ylsa. I should have caught the resemblance." Valam fled to the middle of the encampment, waiting for a thing that did not come. Puzzled, he waited, quickly walking away as Father Jacob approached

He sought refuge not in his own tent, but in another on the far side of camp. He did not seek out Evgej, or Seth, or even Liyan. His search led him directly to another. He did not pause at her door or announce his arrival. Actually, he did not even think anyone would be there. He was shocked to find someone was indeed in the tent.

"You need not lower your eyes," spoke Tsandra, whispering to his thoughts. "I have no secrets."

"I am sorry. I did not think—"

"Yes, I know. Just wait one moment. No need to leave. I shall only be a moment," said Tsandra without even a trace of embarrassment in her words. She stepped into her woolen robe, and then slipped on her boots. She smiled at Valam's wide eyes and bade him to sit. "Your thoughts read like an open book. I thought the time before last when we spoke that we discussed that problem of yours."

"I—I—guess we did," answered Valam. "Wait, wait a minute. This is not what I came here to talk about, so don't lead me astray."

"Well—"

"I understand now what you said to me as our journey began; though, to be honest with you, at the time I did not."

"I thought you would come to understand it, but isn't your timing a little off? Is this why you walked out of council?"

Valam glared back at her and asked, "You can't read what I am thinking right now. Can you?"

"Yes, you are still embarrassed, but I think it will pass."

"That's precisely it," replied Valam, confused.

Tsandra sensed the falseness of his words but did not know what made them false. She wondered what he was hiding from her. Carefully, she prodded his mind while she smiled at him, and she grinned even wider as he smiled back. She found no hidden walls in his center, yet there was something she could not see.

"Why did you do it?" asked Valam.

"Do what?"

"Why did you gather your forces? Was it really for the queen? Or was it over me?"

Now Tsandra comprehended where he was going with his interrogation. "It was for the Queen-Mother; I feared for her safety. I am a warrior; mine is to protect."

"No. The order of the Red are the protectors. Is this not so?"

"It is the right of the Brown to protect also."

"But you protect your people, do you not? You hold the Queen-Mother in check. Is this not so?"

"Where do you get the audacity to speak of such things to me?"

"Is this not so?"

"I think you should leave."

"I will go nowhere!"

"Leave, or I will kill you, myself."

Valam removed his sword from its sheath, and stood eyeing her intent. He considered her words, her tone of voice, and her stance. She did not stand at the ready like one who was willing or wanting to fight. He turned his blade around and handed her the hilt end. "Do me in if you will," said Valam kneeling down on one knee and bowing his head, an act he knew would infuriate the heart of any warrior, no matter their origin.

"I would not strike you down in such a way. Do you think me so treacherous?"

"No, I do not think there is treachery in you, but perhaps you could find the truth and share it with me."

Tsandra was stumped. Where had the questions come from so suddenly, and why now? She had not meant it to come to this. She had merely done what needed to be done, nothing more, so why did it now smite her in the face. She did not make it secret this time that she wished to enter his thoughts. She burst into his mind, seeking to tear it apart and search his every thought but was repelled from the emptiness she found. Again, angrily, she forced her will into his mind. Her eyes went wide with fury.

"It wasn't any of those things, was it?" asked Valam, oblivious to her will upon him.

"Get out!" she yelled, reaching out with all her wrath, again forgetting to enclose its reaches.

"I will not, not until I hear the truth. Tell me, Tsandra of the Brown. Find the words in your heart of hearts and speak them to me."

"I don't know what you are saying."

"The time for playing games with me is over. I remember. I remember it all."

"Oh, really. You remember what?"

"Do not be coy with me! I am asking you in all honesty. I believe you want to tell me the truth, but what keeps your tongue in check?"

"That would be me," spoke Liyan stepping into the tent.

"How long have you been standing out there?" asked Tsandra.

"Only a few moments, but I know of what you speak. I heard the name you spoke, though I think others did not catch it. I don't even think Tsandra heard it."

"What name are you referring to?"

"Why the name of Ekharn the old, of course?"

"Where did you learn it?" asked Tsandra, confusion showing on her face.

"In a dream of sorts."

"A dream, or was it Seth?" asked Liyan, searching Valam's thoughts as he asked it.

Valam stood there staring at Liyan for a time before he responded, but his words were cut short by another. "No, it was not I, brother. You should know I would not speak of such."

"Tell us of this dream, if you may," asked Liyan, yet speaking aloud.

"I don't think I may, Brother Liyan."

Liyan furrowed his brow, but did not reply to Valam; in thought, he told the others what he knew about Valam's words and about Brother Ontyv's visit. Tsandra's response was only a passing complaint, but Seth's was anger, anger so strong it turned his face livid. "Please sit, sit all," begged Tsandra. "Let us talk as friends, as we are all friends in this room."

Tsandra continued to speak, but not aloud; now she carefully thought to enclose her words only to those around her. "Ours is a tale best left untold, but I will say you are correct in your words, Prince Valam Alder."

"Yes," added Liyan, "the Brown began from tragedy and necessity, and so you see, not all our past is bright and glorious either. We, like your kind, also came upon many turnings during the dark times, times that are possibly upon us once more, but now I think we have a correct balance."

"She said there were two queens and two kings," said Valam, slipping, moving his thoughts into words.

"She?" asked Seth, and lagging only moments behind him, Liyan stated the same thing.

"The past is best left to remain in the past. Let us progress not regress. I will be honest with you and say Brother Ontyv did come to send your people home, for this is what the Queen-Mother wished. She did not want you to go home to your lands, and to your fate, for she had altered your fate already in bringing you here at the first. She did not want it to return at the last. I am afraid in so doing, she has upset the balance, and many dark things have come to pass in your lands. For this we are forever sorrowful, Prince Valam."

"No," said Valam, his voice full of wisdom as he spoke, "the balance is brought back in check. Our past is also catching up to us."

"You, my friend, have learned much."

"Yes, and no."

"What will you do now? Will you return to your home? Or will you stay?"

"I do not know, to tell you the truth. I must think, and there are several I must confer with before I decide."

"Father Jacob is a wise man. He will know what is right for you where we may not. Go and talk to him."

"I was not referring to Jacob. Do you know where I can find Teren?"

"Teren?" asked Tsandra, "Why, whatever for?"

"I know where Teren is," said Seth. "He arrived in camp only a short time ago and he asked for you, but at that time I did not know where you were, and I only now recalled his inquiry to mind."

"Yes, I would. Seth, thank you," said Valam rushing out without even saying good-bye. His exodus led him back to his own tent, where he hoped to find Teren waiting. He wasn't surprised to find another there. Valam closely inspected Jacob's demeanor before he said a word. What followed was largely an apology and a subtle explanation, neither of which actually said anything.

Luckily, Father Jacob was clever enough to see through it all to find understanding, the only thing he had hoped to attain. The two sat regarding each other for a time and then Jacob left, departing just as Teren found his way to Valam's quarters. Teren entered without announcement and without offering greetings to Jacob. Neither was surprised to hear an alarm sound throughout the camp moments later. Riders had been spotted approaching from the north, a large group by all accounts.

Chapter Twenty

One day passed without concern, and a second; now thoughts switched to their arrival at Krepost', which would be soon. Xith considered the time lost as a whole, and he figured that they were now several days behind schedule, perhaps more. He took into consideration the rains of the previous days and their directions. They would have to push hard, very hard, for he knew that soon the storms would arrive, and with them passage to the north would come to an end until the seasons changed.

Strangely, they met their first travelers along the road this day, which was not entirely coincidence. Casually, nonchalantly, they greeted each other as they passed. The caravan consisted of many wagons. Xith counted twelve in all as the last one creaked on by. Adrina was unusually excited as she watched them cross alongside the carriage through her small peephole. Nijal was still halfway between sleep and consciousness despite Adrina's nudging and did not wake fully until much later.

Adrina rested her hands on her stomach. She thought back, trying to remember how much time had passed, how long it had been since she'd met the Dragon King. There were many things she did not know, but the one thing she did know was that

Tnavres's presence was both a curse and a blessing. When she took the tiny dragon, she thought her move bold until the Dragon King mocked her saying, "As if you had a choice."

The Dragon King also told her that one of them would be his regardless of what they did. Matched doors of black and white were the final test. White was supposed to bring the hope of life; black death. She chose black; Vilmos chose white. The dragon's milk later saved Valam from the deadly poison and perhaps cursed him. The dragon's milk later saved her and perhaps cursed her as well.

Feeling overwhelmed by all these thoughts, she snuggled tightly into the corner, drinking in the warmth against her hands, sending back feelings of joy and happiness. She dozed off to a light sleep, which did not come without dreams. When she awoke, Nijal's eyes upon her seemed to delve into her very soul and as she looked up with sleep still in her eyes, she was startled. She shrank back as he reached out his hand to her until her wits were fully gathered. "Nijal, I am sorry. I thought it was—oh, never mind. I'm starving. When will we stop for lunch?"

"We already did. I am sorry I did not wake you. You looked so peaceful sleeping, I did not want to disturb you."

Adrina frowned and rubbed her belly. Nijal was hesitant, but eventually produced a small basket, which had been tucked beneath his discarded cloak. Adrina was quick to snatch it up and devour most of its contents, saving only two apples. She gave one to Nijal as her way of saying thanks, and because he was looking hungrily at them in her hands. "Apples, I love apples!" exclaimed Adrina. "Where did you get them?"

"On a little sojourn through the wilderness three days ago."

"Late apples are the best, sweet and tangy, with a coat thick and crunchy!"

The great road took a turn to the north as evening fell upon them at a crossroads of sorts. Many paths seemed to sprout not far from the point where they had chosen to camp for the night. Some were old and largely overgrown. Others were apparently very well traveled; neither weed nor bush could be seen, at least as far as they could see or as far as they dared to venture. They were sure, though, that they were on the right path, for the great road had many characteristics that marked it, and they had been waiting now for several days for it to take its gradual turn to the north.

Neither Xith nor Noman liked the feel of the place they were in, and so they set a double watch this night. With so many to choose from, it had been two nights since Nijal last sat the watch. He took first watch, weary as he was, without complaint. He had only wanted to rest and to close his eyes, but he would have to hold off for two more hours.

Time dragged on slowly for him, but at least he was able to carry on a fragmented conversation with Shchander. Before he knew it, he was lying down to rest. Shalimar and another relieved the two, and after them Amir and Trailer took over. Trailer was a nickname for one of Shchander's men, who was most often found as the last man in the group; thus he had gained the name Trailer.

For the most part Shchander's men were very tight lipped. They held to the code of the warrior and the free man, and they took their responsibilities very seriously. Shchander, as their leader, was their voice and acted as such. The only person who appeared to be put off by their silence, and quite visibly so, was Adrina. She had taken a liking to Shalimar in an odd sort of way, and he had taken much abuse for his previous thoughtlessness. Amir smiled as he thought of Adrina, and soon he pictured another in his thoughts. The last two on watch were Xith and Noman, against the wishes of all present, who contended there was no need.

Xith was cheerful as morning came but withdrawn to his thoughts. After a meager breakfast, Amir and several others went for a short hunt, which they should have done the previous night but had delayed. Soon, after cleaning their catch this day, they were putting distance between themselves and the place where they had camped.

The air was cool and as they now moved through an area populated largely of oak, the rustle of crunching leaves beneath them was the predominant sound. For the most part, the trees were bare now, with few leaves that sought to hang on against the wishes of Mother-Earth. Some grew thankful for the sight of pine, which never lost its color. Its green appeared brighter amidst the brown.

Noman watched Amir very carefully this day. He saw the tension in his muscles, which Amir sought to ease by flexing and massaging. Noman watched Amir play as if he held a blade in his hand, sweeping slowly about his body. Noman knew this was more than just practice or unease. Amir's senses were very keen, and when he was agitated, the waiting preyed heavily upon him.

Noman kept fully alert this day.

Just before mid-day, they happened upon a traveler who journeyed alone. The man turned out to be a minstrel of sorts, and he passed a short while with them playing songs: songs of the sea beyond the forest and the city in the mountain, of green sky and blue lands. He was a pleasant fellow, and they paid him no heed, which was odd in itself. The singer never offered his name, nor did they ask. Neither did he ask for theirs, although in passing he did mention the name of Krepost', the aerie on high.

Xith turned cheerful thoughts now to the path that lay ahead of them. He had not been in the fair city in such a long time that he had forgotten the laughter and mirth it held, which was in strong contrast to its sister city deep within the forest. Even Noman recalled the place with fondness. Although he had not been there in a long time, he did not think it had changed much.

Their camp this evening stood light, with only a single watchman. A low fire burned in a small hearth throughout the night. High overhead even the stars came out in force with a near-perfect moon in their midst. Amir passed the guard off to Shalimar who in turn gave it to Trailer, and then to Nijal; and if Nijal had known better, he would have counted the hours of his watch.

The day arrived with a bit of rain. Although it was mostly a fine mist, it held a hint of ice. After a sluggish start and a short hunt, they returned to their path. They soon found themselves near the edges of the Krasnyj in a place where it raged in full fury, a sign that they were close to the fabled city. They took a much-needed reprieve alongside the cool, actually icy, waters, but they bathed and filled containers just the same.

Adrina also seized the opportunity to rid herself of the filth of travel, and bathed in a secluded pool with only Amir to watch over her. He promised he wouldn't look. Adrina bade him to turn his back nonetheless. The cold water took mental coaxing to enter, but she did, and once she was within it, it did not seem so uncomfortable.

She leaned back, rinsing her hair. Pleasant, peaceful thoughts flowed through her mind. When she opened her eyes moments later she was shocked to see Tnavres withdrawn from her and in the water beside her. She wasn't sure if the tiny dragon was swimming or floundering, but she stood and plucked him from the water all the same, chastising him with her finger.

"Return," she commanded in a harsh whisper. Tnavres glared at her, then locked his jaws around her hand. As his teeth plunged inward, the flesh of her hand turned to stone. She gripped her forearm and squeezed with all her might, trying to stop the progression.

"No, no, no," she whispered as tears streaked down her cheeks.

"You don't listen," came the voice.

"But I have listened. I gave you all I could. What more can I give?"

"Tnavres will tell you when it is time. Do as you've been told."

"No," she whispered.

Tnavres entered her angrily, letting her know the force of his will. He sank into the flesh of her upturned palm, swept up within her arm and crossed her innards to his resting place in her belly. His mark was upon her right palm now where she could look upon it and remember.

Adrina found that getting out of the water was even more difficult than entering. The air was colder against her skin than the water, and she did not wish to leave it, as much as she tried. "Amir," she called out softly, but when he did not turn, she said it again louder, "Amir!"

"Yes," he said turning around.

"Turn back around!"

"My dear, what is it you wish of me?" asked Amir, knowing exactly what Adrina wanted.

"Please hand me my wraps and without looking."

"I told you I won't look."

"Just give them to me," said Adrina standing up, reaching out to get the cloak Amir had in his hands. Amir made her walk a few steps to get them before he finally gave them to her. A smile lit his face as he turned away. Adrina's face was flushed with both embarrassment and anger. He thought it suited her nicely.

Adrina glared at him, and stomped back to where the others waited for her and Amir. "A little bit of privacy!" shouted Adrina as she retreated into the coach, throwing down its shades and locking the doors. Amir approached Xith. With a grin still on his lips, he went up to the carriage door and knocked on it two times.

"What! What?" shouted Adrina, not opening the door.

"You'll want these," said Amir.

Adrina peeked out the window to see what he held, and then threw the door open. She was quick to grab the remainder of her belongings and then in anger, she touched her right hand to his shoulder. Amir chuckled, a deep, rolling laugh. The sound began as a trickle, and just as it rose, it stopped. Amir flexed his shoulders, and rolled his head to ease the stiffness.

He dropped to one knee as he fought to draw his sword. "Noman!" he strained to scream, but nothing issued forth. An icy hand dealt him another blow, this time to the left shoulder. He turned his head to look at the creature he perceived behind him just as it stepped forward.

Pain shot through his legs, then his back, and finally his arms. Wildly, he flailed the air using the last of his strength to lash out. He fell backwards to the ground with a thud, striking his head against the coach as he went down. As his world faded to darkness, Adrina closed the door to the coach.

Chapter Twenty One

Stone walls rose high and sheer about them. Calyin, Midori, and Edwar Serant wound their way among the many turns, delving deep into the shadows. A soft tapping sound followed their path, high above, though none below knew it. They walked in a single column with Midori to the fore and Serant to the rear, each leading one of the horses. They held to a slow, steady pace, carefully picking their way among the rocks and crevices. Frequently, they thought of Geoffrey and Captain Brodst.

Ahead the canyon appeared to end in a solid rock wall, but still they made their way toward it, seemingly inch by inch. Lord Serant followed the lee of the river, not paying heed to the wall's proximity to them. The churning of the water spoke volumes to him. Somewhere in front of them, the river's path turned downward.

The river gradually cut a deep course into the rock and a distance of only a few feet separated them from the waters. As the depth gradually increased, Lord Serant began to move away from the river's edge, and it was here that he first noticed the etchings into the rock. A shallow path of sorts had been carved out of the rocks through years of wear. The path ran smooth and straight. He regarded it as a roadway of sorts and supposed that long ago this path had been heavily traveled.

Some hours later they stopped to gather their bearings and to provide tired bodies with a bit of nourishment. The sheer wall looming immediately before them, jagged, tall and insurmountable, was perhaps an additional reason they had decided to stop. Here the trail ended, but they did not acknowledge its presence.

A high, shrill sound from high above startled them, and all conversation stopped. The three drew their blades and watched, waiting as many figures slithered down ropes in front of them and to either side. Those across the river they did not fear, for they saw no way for them to traverse it, so they turned toward the others. Slowly, they sought to retreat.

Serant flailed out with his foot, only to come upon empty air. He cocked his head back, and half turned to look. He saw the river swirling with white waters well below him. He turned quickly back to face those approaching with his eyes continually darting to the two at his side. A gleam, a glitter, he caught in Midori's eyes, and anger was upon her face. She held her long dagger before her without wavering. Calyin gripped her blade with nervous hands, but she did not lower it as those that came closer demanded.

Lord Serant looked again to Calyin and then to Midori. He quietly told them that should all else fail, the river was their safest route, no matter their thoughts on the subject. He touched Calyin's hand one last time, and then moved forward two steps. Calyin moved towards him, but he pushed her back. "And just where will you be?" said Calyin into Serant's ear.

"Lower your blades, we mean you no harm. We only wish to separate you from your purse, and then we will leave you."

"Do as I say!" said Serant, hurriedly.

"I will not go," returned Calyin.

"Tsk tsk!" shouted the man who now stood directly in front of Lord Serant; only their blades separated them.

"Just what is it you want?" asked Serant, in a haughty deep bass.

"Only your gold, nothing more, nothing less!"

"You may have all the gold we carry if you leave us now."

"Give it to me, and we shall leave. You have my word."

"A word is a bond, is it not?" asked Serant, moving back a short pace.

"Why, of course, of course. If a man cannot keep a promise, he is not a man."

Lord Serant fumbled through his cloak and retrieved a small leather pouch, which he tossed to the man. The man sheathed his sword, untied the small purse, and emptied the coins into his hand, counting each in turn, and shaking his head at each. "Surely you have more than this?"

"That is all the gold I have."

"What of the ring on your finger and the gem on the crown of the hilt of your sword?"

"They are not gold."

"Ah yes, but are they not worth their weight in gold?" questioned the man, raising his blade again.

"Midori, I trust Calyin's life in your hands. Do what you

must!" called Serant pushing Calyin into Midori. He lowered his eyes to the waters of the river only for an instant, and then whispered, "I am sorry," as he pushed them both over the edge, and into the waiting waters.

"Bad, very bad. I do not like that, and when I do not like something, I usually kill the offender."

"Just as well. Today is a good day to die!" shouted Serant charging the man.

"Not likely—" spoke the man as he called to his confederates.

Lord Serant struggled under the weight of a heavy blow, and for an instant he stared through crossed blades into his opponent's eyes. Only then did it become obvious to him that the man he faced was oblivious to his lineage, and perhaps he truly only wished his valuables, but Serant would not part with them. There were only a few tangible things he valued above all, and one was the ring that had been passed down through generations from father to son, and the other the sword of his forefathers.

"One against dozens!" shouted a voice, yet a good distance away, "Not very fair at all!" Captain Brodst and Geoffrey wasted no time in their charge, sending men scrambling to avoid being trampled by horses' hooves. Geoffrey raised his mount on its hind-legs just to the right of the one Serant fought, while Brodst offered a hand to Lord Serant. "We could not leave you, my friend. The farther we drew away from you, the heavier our hearts grew. Come, let us be off!"

The two horsemen made a quick, decisive retreat. Lord Serant looked back, fixing upon the upturned face. "Another day!"

called out Serant, "Another day!" The man sheathed his weapon and then turned his back to them. He did not order his men to pursue because he knew the time of their next meeting would be sooner than the other thought. Serant watched as the attackers withdrew, climbing back up their ropes.

"Your timing couldn't have been better!" exclaimed Serant patting Brodst on the back.

"Where are Calyin and Midori?"

Lord Serant brought a hand to his chin, "Oh my—" he thought. "The water—they are in the river."

"The river?"

"Yes, the river. I didn't see any other way."

Geoffrey and Brodst began to laugh because for a moment it seemed funny; but the feeling passed, and it suddenly was not humorous any more. Lord Serant scoured his thoughts, searching for a quick solution, which did not come. At the time, it had seemed his only choice, but now he knew it was a brash act. He did not like to think that he was a fool.

"What in the name of the Father is that?" exclaimed Captain Brodst reining in his mount suddenly, so suddenly that Lord Serant almost lost his grip.

"That is not of the Father, of this I can assure you," replied Geoffrey. Even though he could not clearly see those that readily approached, he recognized them. He knew nothing good would come of their meeting. The hunter beasts had only one thought on their minds, and that was their prey. Geoffrey and Brodst began to turn their mounts around, back in the direction they had come; midway, they realized their dilemma.

Neither Captain Brodst nor Lord Serant had seen anything like these before, but immediately they sensed danger and instinctively they reacted. Geoffrey bade them to return their weapons to their sheaths; as much as he hated to admit it, he knew this was an encounter they would lose, and he knew this as surely as he lived and breathed. A tiny voice in his mind hoped that perhaps they were not the objects of the beasts' hunt, in which case they had nothing to fear.

As the creatures drew closer, their distinctive features became quite noticeable. They had the appearance of men, but a thick, fur-covered hide enshrouded their forms. Their faces were long with an elongated snout, and white upturned fangs sprouted from their mouths. Even at a distance, Geoffrey could see crystalline droplets ooze from the nearest creature's mouth, a sign that he was looking for.

Geoffrey yelled for the captain to follow him and then retreated back down the canyon, the way they had come. Very soon they found themselves approaching the high canyon walls. Those waiting above rejoiced at the sighting, and one in particular had a broad grimace on his face. "Welcome back!" called out a now familiar voice.

"What do we do?" asked Brodst.

"This is not good, definitely not good."

"No, it is not."

As they turned their mounts around to face those that came up from behind them, the ravine, wherein lay the river, caught their eye, and more importantly the sound of rushing water caught their ear. Geoffrey did a mental calculation. He approximated the bandits' numbers to be around twenty or perhaps a little more. He also knew their kind well enough to know a small reserve was probably waiting. It was at least a two-to-one ratio.

He turned back toward the leader of the bandits. He wanted to get close enough to recognize the clan, but this was also his gravest mistake. As he staggered forward, the distances closed between the two forces. They found themselves in the middle of a stand-off, and he knew they were the prize.

The pack leader of the hunters, who identified himself to the bandit chief as Ermog, dismounted at a careful distance and approached singly. He called the bandit chief to a council of words, and though he spoke in the tongue of man, his speech was slurred and did not carry well. Only the other's words carried fully to their ears, and it was these words that sparked Geoffrey's interest.

In the interim, he conversed with Serant and Brodst, speaking quietly, stopping as the two spoke, and starting again in low whispers, passing his concerns on to them. The bandit leader had recognized Geoffrey and thus discovered the identities of those that accompanied him. He was playing with Ermog for the price of the bounty. Geoffrey knew the teachings of the histories and the passing down of the sons of the fathers and the realms, but the Borderlands were a realm outside all else. Nowhere did the histories speak of the Bandit Kingdoms or the Hunter Clan, societies that were older than that of the Great Kingdom but had never gained recognition in civilized circles.

Geoffrey understood the references to blood and sword, coin

and fist, and as the two leaders returned to their ranks, he knew what he must do. He dismounted slowly, signaling for Serant and Brodst to do the same. He made sure they made no sudden movements, and he maintained his speech in low whispers. After a close but limited survey of the ledge and the waters below, they jumped, hoping and believing the river would carry them away to safety.

Chapter Twenty Two

Valam waited patiently for Mikhal and Danyel' to return with the scouting party. The group of riders, anticipated to be large, turned out to be only the small band that had been dispatched earlier and a large group of strayed horses. His eyes lit as he saw Mikhal and Danyel' race their mounts toward the place where he waited. He did not waste any time with pleasantries and quickly invited the two to accompany him.

The three went to Valam's quarters, where Teren yet waited without saying a word to anyone else. Teren listened intently as Valam spoke to the others, waiting for the correct time to speak his mind also.

"Prince Valam, if I may interrupt for a moment. You are missing the most important point. The four of us were given the gift of sight for a reason, a very specific reason. We merely saw you move through the steps. You must decide for yourself, but remember this in your decision. Choose your path with great care and follow it through to its completion."

"I wish I knew for sure," quietly whispered Valam. "I always pictured Captain Evgej and Seth at my side, no offense—"

"The future has many turnings. Perhaps it will be so. Perhaps we play a part in the paths of your future, or maybe we are your turning points in the path."

"That is a curious statement, Brother Teren," said Danyel'.

Two days passed and still Valam struggled with the choices in his mind. He knew not which direction to take. Thoughts of home appealed to him even though he knew the dangers that awaited him if he returned. This day weighed heavily on him. Teren returned to the plains, which were now completely buried beneath a very thick blanket of snow. Even the coastal areas received a fair amount.

The sky overhead promised that today would be clear and cloudless, and it was with a heavy heart that Valam returned to the affairs of the camp. The cold spell had left its mark on the camp, and supplies of wood for their fires were now depleted once again. They also had to face the fact that many months of cold might lay ahead, and the tents would not make this hardship any easier. They needed to find adequate shelter.

The small villages of the plains now lay deep in snow also, but the heart of the plain was not where they wished to go. The cold was just tolerable here; there it would be more than unbearable. They needed to find a better solution and soon. The cove where their ships were moored was suggested by Father Jacob, and Liyan also seemed to think this would be a good choice as it was partially sheltered from the winds and close enough that the move would not be excessively taxing.

The move began slowly and for a brief period it kept everyone occupied. Teren returned during the interim and took Danyel' and Mikhal away with him. When the change of camps was completed, Valam came to the hard decision to use their remaining wagons as the source for their fires. He vowed even if they had to start burning the longboats they would always have a fire in each hearth through the cold nights.

Valam stood still, oblivious to the light drizzle falling around him. His thoughts were heavy and his mood decidedly stern. He muddled over words he must speak when he returned to where the others waited. Jacob called a second meeting to solve their current problems and to find insight on the direction they were moving. Inside, all sat waiting; even the seven lieutenants were present. Seth ventured out into the elements, finding Valam gazing fixedly at some distant point that was probably only known to Valam. Seth knew and understood Valam's situation. He had discussed this at length with Liyan over the past several days, and he knew Valam actually didn't have a choice to make but rather to accept.

Valam hadn't even turned to acknowledge the presence beside him although he had noticed. His voice began softly, gaining volume only as it reached the final syllable. "—I must return to Leklorall and from there, perhaps home—"

"Yes, I know."

"I wanted to tell you before I told the others."

"You need not explain. I understand. I will miss you heartily."

The two stood silent for a long time before they joined the others in the meeting. Father Jacob was pleased to see the two enter together. As Jacob took his place at the table, Valam looked to each face around the room, recalling the names of each as he did so. Brother Liyan had donned the gray of his office; Tsandra was arrayed in brown; even Seth, Valam noted for the first time, wore the red of his order; and Teren wore black.

Cagan was not in attendance, but Valam had not expected to see him here, with ships so close by. Stretched out in a line to the right of Captain Mikhal sat the seven lieutenants. Valam looked puzzled for a moment upon seeing two empty chairs in the far corner before he recalled who was not present.

He crossed to the head position without further delay. His mind stumbled and stuttered, as did his tongue, as he began to speak. "Father Jacob, Brother Liyan, Brother Seth—as all of you know, I have been quite pensive as of late. It is very difficult to hide the discontent of your heart. Oftentimes the facts speak for themselves, and as I have considered the many things that are ahead for all of us here, I have stumbled over a host of obstacles, which were mostly phantoms of my own creation. I soon realized I really only had one choice to make, and this did not come without the help of a very close friend—and just a few, short moments ago—"

"Storm approaching!" interrupted the page as he burst into the tent.

"Will we never get this meeting completed?" asked Jacob, raising his eyes, and speaking upward.

"Storm?"

"Yes, sir, a storm—"

"Shoo, shoo, go back to where you came from. Go on, Prince Valam, please finish. Wait, wait, wait, one minute there—pass the word to raise stocks high in case the snows are severe and to prepare for the cold—"

"Yes, sir—but begging your pardon, of course, you don't understand."

"And just what don't I understand?" asked Jacob with more vehemence than he intended.

"Nothing, Father. May I return to my duties?"

"Yes, go!"

The page departed with an appearance of defeat on his face. Father Jacob shook his head and then reclaimed his seat. Valam hesitantly began again although he paused long to recall where he had left off. Now the import of what he had been carefully building up to seemed trivial, so he just came out and said what he intended to do.

"I must return to Leklorall, for only there, I believe, will I find the answers I seek. From there, I may perhaps find that I need to return to Great Kingdom."

Surprised gasps issued from many, quickly followed by a loud murmuring. A few, like Father Jacob, had been expecting it, and the anxiety of waiting to actually hear it was finally released. Valam was most surprised by Teren's response, which was disbelief. He had received a similar response from Mikhal, which he counted as disappointment.

"I will select a small group to accompany me, but I will only take those who willingly choose to return with me."

"I do not think that will be a problem, your highness," said Redcliff. Danyel' immediately responded with a wide grimace and a sharp glare, forcing silence upon those around him. Valam started to speak again but stopped abruptly as Evgej entered.

"Didn't the page reach you?"

"Yes, he did, and as a matter of fact, he just left. Don't worry, captain, we are well prepared for the snow. We have already made provisions."

"Snow? No, Prince Valam, the storm comes from the sea. Cagan is extremely worried."

"This cove should harbor us from the worst. We will be safe."

"I am not so sure. Perhaps you had better accompany me."

Father Jacob stood with a pained look stretched across his features and approached. He spoke in low whispers to the two, carrying them off a short distance to the corner. When he finished, he excused himself from the meeting and accompanied Evgej outside, leaving Valam behind, very confused.

As Valam walked to the front of the table and stared into the eyes of those about him, worry and fear touched him. Jacob's words played in his mind, "You must decide now," he had said, "you must decide now or it will be too late." Jacob already knew what the winds carried toward them.

"I think the time has come, the time when I must leave. I must return to Leklorall before the sun sets this day. There are powerful forces at work here both for and against us. Brother Teren, Brother Tsandra, I would have you accompany me if you would."

Valam ignored the pointed remarks that jumped into his thoughts mid-stream and continued. "Brother Seth and Brother Liyan, I regret that I think your place is here for now. Lieutenant Eran, you think I don't remember your name, but I do. Willam the Black, Pavil the Bearded, S'tryil, Son of Lord S'tryil of High

Province, Ylsa, sister to Eran, and Tae, Master of Redcliff, your places are here, save you, S'tryil."

Valam regarded S'tryil for a moment. "I shall need a new captain, and you shall be the one. Captain Mikhal and Lieutenant Danyel' shall accompany me. Father Jacob and Evgej shall remain."

S'tryil waited until it appeared that Valam was finished speaking before he responded. "I cannot accept the honor bestowed upon me. I request that you pass the rank of captain to Ylsa. She has already earned it."

"Lieutenant Ylsa's time will be soon; your time is now, Captain S'tryil. Take command of your men and follow Father Jacob's instructions."

Valam continued to ignore Teren and Tsandra's remarks, which hit him full, even as he walked away. The wind outside, a strong breeze, immediately assaulted his senses, carrying with it sand and debris from around the camp. Valam had to shield his eyes with his arm to see clearly. He was amazed at the speed with which the storm raged towards them.

"Prince Valam, wait!" came the plea into his thoughts, even as he fought to seal them.

"I do not have time to waste! Tell the others to meet the long boat crew and go out to the flagship. She is Cagan's favorite, or so I have heard."

"They spoke nothing of Tsandra. Why is she—"

"Perhaps I have my own reasons. Now please hurry!" shouted Valam.

"Valam wait!"

The voice aloud caught Valam by surprise for an instant until he recognized it. "Yes, Captain Mikhal, take the lieutenant's detachment to the flag ship. Cagan is already there."

"But they are not—"

"Yes, I know," replied Valam as he walked away.

"Yes," returned Valam in thought as yet another voice disturbed him. Tsandra was quick to pick the thought from his center. "How many?" she asked. "The choice is yours," he replied.

Valam was interrupted one more time on the way to his tent, but this intrusion did not bother him. He and Seth had been through a lot together and to part now when they had come so far seemed ironic. But sometimes, thought Valam, "Irony was truth." And so when all preparations were made, he watched Cagan's steady hand lead the ship into the tack, turning back only after great hesitation.

"Goodbye," he whispered in his thoughts to Seth, Liyan and the others. "I have faith we will see each other again soon."

Chapter Twenty Three

"Amir, Amir? Can you hear me? Answer me."

"Noman?"

"No, I am Xith. Welcome back; you just sit there. You have been under too much strain lately. You will ride in the coach today and rest."

"Xith?"

"Yes, you just rest now, everything will be fine."

"Where is Noman?"

"Never mind, you just rest there a moment more."

Xith indicated that Shchander and Nijal should help Amir into the carriage now. The two did as they were bid, but it took a third to bear such an enormous burden. Nijal grabbed Amir on the left, Shchander on the right, and Trailer took the feet, stepping into the coach first and then carefully turning with the others to carry Amir inside.

The pace was lethargic this day as anticipation grew to a new high. The road joined with the great river and now ran along its course. Krepost' lay a day away at best and soon the sea would separate them from the lands of East and West. Noman turned to thoughts of supplies they would need for the north, and while the others turned to thoughts of Krepost', a song sprang to their lips.

Adrina stared fixedly at Amir with open concern upon her face. She watched him for a time, growing restless, and finally turning her attentions to the scenery around her. She could hear the churning of water even over the rolling of the wagon's wheels and the clippety-clop of the horses' hooves. A voice startled her, and though she knew better, she stuck her head out the window, looking for the speaker.

"You would do best to turn around, friends," rang the lofty voice.

"Turn around?" asked Xith. "Why whatever for?"

"And what makes us your friends?" asked Nijal.

"Whoa, hold on there. You be talking to old Kelar. I can see clearly you are from the west and have traveled far, so I will tell you this: 'tis not a good time to be happening upon our fair city."

Noman smiled and considered the words before responding. "We will watch our path, friend Kelar, thanks." Kelar just waved and continued on his way. The others in his party passed without saying a word. Xith turned to Noman and raised an eyebrow. He was glad to know some things didn't change. The people of Krepost' were still as odd and unpredictable as he recalled them.

Hours later, after several stops, the descending sun on the horizon lighted a most magnificent sight. High upon a steep bluff with cliff walls cascading down to meet the bay sat the city of Krepost', coming into view at long last. The only road that cut its way to the top of the aerie lay just across the river. The distance they needed to traverse and the climb would unfortunately cost them several hours of toil before this day was over, but they would gladly pay the price.

A cool breeze came in across the bay on a direct westerly course, bringing with it an odor of salt that assaulted the senses. Travel-weary bodies gained a new surge of energy that swept them onward; even the horses seemed to sense a long-deserved rest ahead. Shchander raced Nijal to the river, charging his mount to the very edge of the water.

The two stood there, waiting for the others to catch up. Nijal considered the promise he had made to himself some weeks ago when the nine men had joined their company. Once they reached the coast, their journey together would end. As he watched Shchander's lighthearted mood, he let the thoughts slip away. He would consider them at another time, perhaps after several days of rest.

Xith reined the horses to a halt, stepped down from the coach, and then walked over to a lantern hanging from a small post. For a moment, he thought about lighting it with a spark of magic, but the idea was short-lived. He retrieved flint and steel and set a spark to the lamp, raising it high above his head, and rotating it from right to left.

In the falling light, he waited for the signal to return, thinking that perhaps the brightness of the setting sun obscured the response. He waited until the sun sank from sight, and then repeated his signal. He paused, waiting patiently, and then handed the lantern to Nijal. Hearts sank after minutes passed with still no response; nonetheless, they waited.

Discouraged, they set up camp without much discussion. The lights of the city pointing the distance canceled any feelings of merriment. This stage of their journey would last one more day, and there was nothing they could do about it although Xith did work up a long list of harsh words to launch at the barge-master.

Amir awoke from a long day's sleep just as the sky was shrouded in darkness. He was still quite groggy as he approached the fire where most were seated. The smell of fish surprised his nostrils. Nijal and Shchander muttered something about idle hands when he inquired where the meal had come from. Stiffly, Amir sat down on the ground. The raging hunger in his belly was quenched, but only after his third helping.

As the time for the first watch arrived and the men began to retire for the evening, Amir offered to take the first watch, claiming he wasn't tired in the least. Shchander, who was supposed to have the first watch anyway, said he would hold the watch with Amir. The sounds around them began to die out, the crackle of the fire was replaced by the swirl of the water, and later the sound of laughter drifted into their ears and into their thoughts.

Shchander turned cold eyes to the glow in the distance. Before the last embers from the fire were extinguished, he stocked and restored it. Soon it was a cheerful blaze once more. A sudden crackling sound from behind him startled Shchander. He stood and walked toward it.

"Don't worry, Shchander. It was nothing."

"But, I thought—"

"Only an animal passing by, come back to the fire."

Shchander sat back down, casting away the dark thoughts in his mind. As the last hour of their watch wore on, the day's travel caught up to Shchander and his eyes grew heavy. He could scarcely hold them open. "Go get some rest. Shalimar will take over in a few minutes—I can sit out the rest by myself," offered Amir, and Shchander accepted. Sleep found him as soon as he put his head down to rest.

Amir never roused Shalimar or anyone else. He sat the guard throughout the hours of darkness. The first shards of morning light found him sitting beside a low fire. His attention was turned toward the black waters where the river joined the bay. He was careful to wake Noman and Xith last.

Breakfast was quick, and most did not eat at all. The ferry came into view just as they broke camp. Xith waited, lantern in hand, closely eyeing the old one who guided those who pushed the barge along its course. As it landed on the shore, Xith blew out the lamp and set it back on its post. He organized the words that gnawed at his thoughts all night. "Hello—" he greeted the barge-master coldly, stopping only to work out his remaining words.

"Well, a good day to you, and such a beautiful day it is. Well, well, what are you waiting for? Come aboard, and I will take you across the river for a pittance."

The warm salutation caused Xith to stumble in venting his wrath and what came out was not what he intended. "And just how much is that going to cost us?"

"Less than you would think, my friend. Come, step aboard, and we'll carry you off to the northern shore. The fair city of Krepost' waits. The market is just awakening. You can catch a fair amount of goods for a goodly sum if you are quick. So you must hurry!"

"Do you wish payment now or later?"

"We'll have time on the river for petty things. Come and listen to the words of an old river man. I'll tell you things you've never heard, and I'll charge you a meager fare, but only for the river's crossing. You need not pay for the words unless you've a mind."

Xith cursed low under his breath and boarded with the others. The barge-master caught the malice in his eyes and was quick to burst into a story and to set the barge on its return course. Thankfully, everyone was able to get onto the ferry without trouble. The river here was quite swift although in this section it was also shallow and was normally turbulent. The raft was of generous proportions.

Four men guided the barge toward the other shore, one in each of its corners, as the master explained its workings, among the many tales he spun in the short time. He explained how the ferry had two landings on the opposite shore and that the easterly one was the one they should wait at on their return route, for the other was just the landing for the return from the southerly shore. He told them how two asses bore the barge back to the departure landing against the river's current and he even worked the sum of their payment into a song.

Feeling sorry for his wry demeanor, Xith dropped twice the necessary coinage into the old man's hands as they disembarked. As he rode away, he glanced back with a hint of laughter yet in his eyes. He watched the two mules pull the ferry along the river's edge. The road to Krepost' was the only path they could follow, and as it was where they were bound for, they took it with great eagerness, following as it slowly wound its way to the top of the bluff.

The answers Xith and Noman sought were beyond Krepost', but for now the small company was safe. The city would house and keep them until they were ready for the next, more dangerous, part of the journey.

End Of Book Three
The Story continues with:
In the Service of Dragons IV

The dragons will be revealed.

ABOUT THE AUTHOR

 Robert Stanek is the author of many previously published books, including several bestsellers. Currently, he lives in the Pacific Northwest with his wife and children. Robert is proud to have served in the Persian Gulf War as a combat crewmember on an electronic warfare aircraft. During the war, he flew numerous combat and combat support missions, logging over two hundred combat flight hours. His distinguished accomplishments during the Persian Gulf War earned him nine medals, including the United States of America's highest flying honor, the Air Force Distinguished Flying Cross.

As a boy, he dreamed of being a writer. In elementary school, he was a junior editor for the school newspaper. Although he has written many books for professionals since 1994, his works of fiction have quickly become his most popular books. His first novel was Keeper Martin's Tale, which was simultaneously released in adult and children's editions. He describes the book as "a story of mystery, intrigue, magic, and adventure." Many of his other works of fiction are also fantasies, set in incredibly fantastic worlds.

Learn more at
www.robertstanek.com

Enter the world of the books
www.ruinmist.com

Characters in the Books

Adrina Alder

Princess Adrina. Third and youngest daughter of King Andrew.

Alexandria Alder

Queen Alexandria. Former Queen of Great Kingdom; Adrina's mother, now deceased.

Amir

One of the lost. Child of the Race Wars. Son of Ky'el, king of the Titans.

Andrew Alder

King Andrew. Ruler of Great Kingdom, first of that name to reign.

Ansh Brodst

Captain Brodst. Former captain of the guard, palace at Imtal. King's Knight Captain.

Anth S'tryil

Bladesman S'tryil is a ridesman by trade but a bladesman of necessity. He is heir to the Great House of S'tryil.

Antwar Alder

King Antwar. The Alder King. First to rule Great Kingdom.

Ashwar Tae

The 12th son of Oshowyn.

Ayrian

Eagle Lord of the Gray Clan.

Brodst, Captain

See Ansh Brodst.

Br'yan, Brother

Elf of the Red order. Proper Elvish spelling is Br'-än.

Cagan

Sailmaster Cagan. Elven ship captain of the Queen's schooner. Proper Elvish spelling is Ka'gan.

Calyin Alder

Princess Calyin. Eldest daughter of King Andrew.

Catrin Mitr

Sister Catrin. Priestess of Mother-Earth.

Charles Riven

King Charles, former ruler of Sever, North Warden of the Word.

Danyel' Revitt

Lieutenant Danyel'. Former Sergeant

	Quashan' garrison.
Delinna Alder	See Midori.
De Vit, Chancellor	See Edwar De Vit.
Der, Captain	See Olev Der.
Edwar De Vit	Chancellor De Vit. King Jarom's primary aid and chancellor.
Edwar Serant	Lord Serant. Husband to Princess Calyin. Governor of High Province, also called Governor of the North Watch.
Edward Tallyback	A troant (half troll, half giant) and friend of Xith's. Edward would be the first to tell you that he is only distantly related to the hideous wood trolls and that he is a direct descendant of swamp trolls.
Eldrick	A tree spirit of old.
Emel Brodstson	Emel. Former guardsman palace at Imtal; Son of Ansh Brodst.
Erravane	Queen of the Wolmerrelle.
Evgej, Captain	See Vadan Evgej.
First Brothers	Council made up of the presiding members of each order of the Elven Brotherhood.
Francis Epart	Father Francis. Member of the priesthood of Great Father.
Galan, Brother	Elf of the Red order, second only to Seth.
Geoffrey Solntse	Lord Geoffrey. Lord of the Free City of Solntse. Descendant of Etyr Solntse, first Lord of Solntse.
Great Father	Father of all. He whom we visit at the last.
Imson Adylton	Captain Adylton. Imtal garrison captain.
Isador Froen d'Ga	Lady Isador. Nanny for Adrina; given honorary title of Lady by King.
Jacob Froen d'Ga	Father Jacob. First minister to the king.

	Head of the priesthood in the capital city of Imtal.
Jarom Tyr'anth	King Jarom, ruler of Vostok, East Warden of the Word.
Jasmine	Sister Jasmine. First priestess of the Mother.
Keeper Martin	See Martin Braddabaggon.
Ky'el	Legendary titan who gave men, elves and dwarves their freedom at the dawn of the First Age.
Lillath Tabborrath	Mother of Vilmos.
Liyan, Brother	Elf, presiding member of East Reach High Council.
Mark, King	The Elven King of West Reach.
Martin Braddabaggon	Keeper Martin. A lore keeper and head of the Council of Keepers.
Michal Klaive	Baron Klaive. Low-ranking nobleman whose lands are rich in natural resources.
Midori	Sister Midori. The name Princess Delinna Alder earned after joining the priestesses.
Mikhal	Captain Mikhal. Quashan' garrison captain.
Misha	Innkeeper, an old friend of Xith's.
Mother-Earth	The great mother. She who watches over all.
Myrial	Adrina's childhood friend. The current Housemistress of Imtal Palace.
Nijal Solntse	First son of Geoffrey, former day captain city garrison, Free City of Solntse.
Niyomi	Beloved of Dalphan, lost in the Blood Wars.
Noman	Master of Amir. Keeper of the City of the Sky.

Olev Der	2nd Captain Olev Der of the Quashan' garrison. Captain of the City Watch.
Parren	Keeper Parren. Member of the Council of Keepers.
Pyetr Brodst	Second son of Captain Ansh Brodst. Guardsman palace at Imtal.
Queen Mother	The Elven Queen. Queen of East Reach, mother of her people.
Q'yer	Keeper Q'yer. Member of the Council of Keepers.
Ry'al, Brother	Elf, second of the Blue. Heir to Samyuehl's gift.
Samyuehl, Brother	Elf, first of the Blue order.
Sathar the Dark	He that returned from the dark journey.
Serant, Lord	See Edwar Serant.
Seth, Brother	Elf, first of the Red, protector of Queen Mother.
Shalimar	A warrior of Shchander's company.
Shchander	Old compatriot of Nijal.
S'tryil, Lieutenant	See Anth S'tryil.
Teren, Brother	Elf of the Brown.
Tnavres	Adrina's dragon.
Trailer	A warrior of Shchander's company.
Tsandra, Brother	Elf, first of the Brown order.
Vadan Evgej	Captain Evgej. Former Swordmaster, city garrison at Quashan'.
Valam	Prince Valam. Governor of South Province. King Andrew's only son. Also known as the Lord and Prince of the South.
Van'te Duardin	Chancellor Van'te. Former first adviser to King Andrew, now confidant to Lord

Valam in South Province.

Vilmos Tabborrath	An apprentice of the forbidden arcane arts.
Vil Tabborrath	Father of Vilmos and village councilor of Tabborrath.
Volnej Eragol	Chancellor Volnej. High Council member, Great Kingdom.
Willam Ispeth	Duke Ispeth. Ruler of the independent Duchy of Ispeth.
William Riven	King William. King of Sever.
Xith	Last of Watchers, Shaman of Northern Reaches. He is most definitely a Gnomic Dwarf (Gnome) though there are those that believe he is a creature of a different sort altogether.
Yi Duardin	Chancellor Yi. First adviser to King Andrew. Brother of Van'te.
Ylad', Brother	Elf, first of the White order.
Ylsa Heman	Bowman first rank. A female archer and later a sectional commander.

Learn more about the people, places and things in Robert Stanek's world of Ruin Mist. Read *Ruin Mist Heroes, Legends & Beyond*—a companion book for *The Kingdoms & the Elves of the Reaches* and *In the Service of Dragons*.

The Reaches

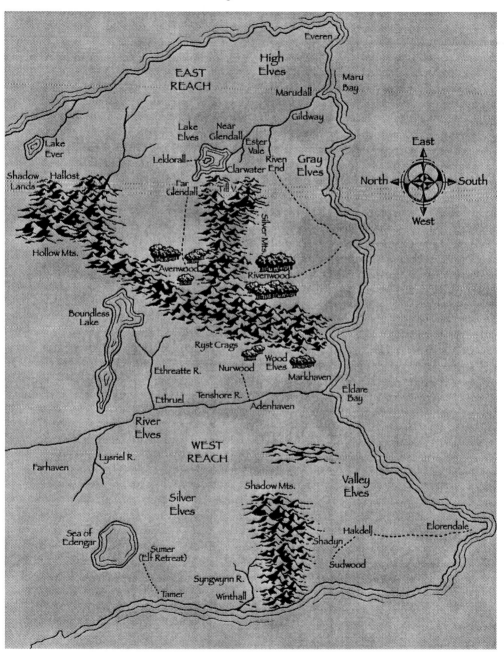

The Kingdoms

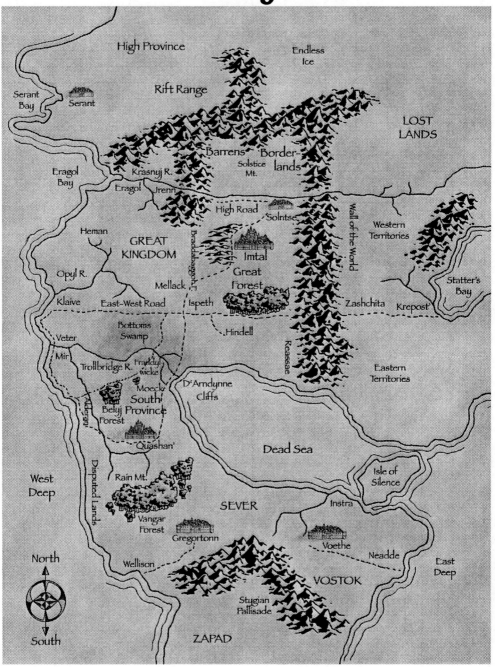

Under-Earth

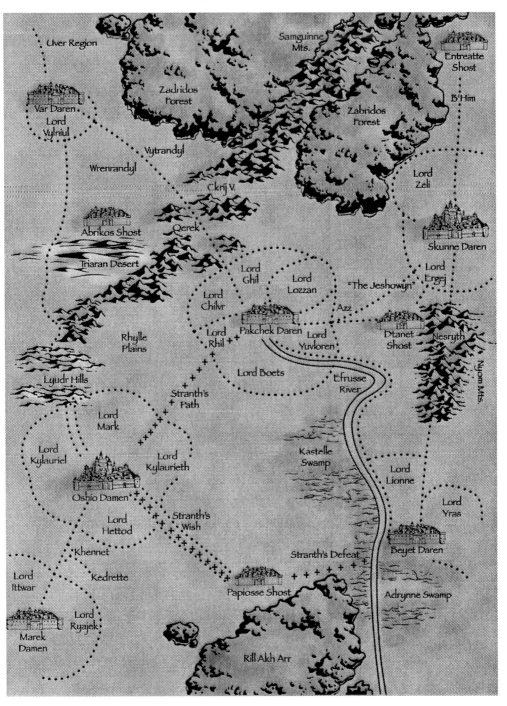

Uver Region

Samguinne Mts.

Entreatte Shost

Zabridos Forest

B'Him

Var Daren Lord Vylniul

Zabridos Forest

Vytrandyl

Lord Zeli

Wrenrandyl

Ckrij V.

Abrikos Shost

Qerek

Skunne Daren

Triaran Desert

Lord Ghil

Lord Lozzan

Lord Ergej

"The Jeshowyn"

Lord Chilvr

Azz

Rhylle Plains

Lord Rhil

Pakchek Daren

Lord Yuvloren

Dtanet Shost

Nesryth

Lord Boets

Efrusse River

Lyudr Hills

Stranth's Path

Lord Mark

Kastelle Swamp

Lord Lionne

Lord Kylauriel

Lord Kylaurieth

Lord Yras

Oshio Damen

Lord Hettod

Stranth's Wish

Beyet Daren

Khennet

Stranth's Defeat

Lord Ittwar

Kedrette

Papiosse Shost

Adrynne Swamp

Lord Ryajek

Marek Damen

Rill Akh Arr

Nyom Mts.

KEEPER MARTIN'S TALES

THE KINGDOMS AND THE ELVES OF THE REACHES

Keeper Martin's Tales

BOOK 1

ROBERT STANEK

The Kingdoms & the Elves of the Reaches

Inside you'll discover the breathtaking world of Ruin Mist where the mystical and the magical abound, and you'll fall in love with a boy who would become a mage, a princess who is just now seeing the world around her, a warrior elf who undertakes an epic journey, and their friends.

The Kingdoms & the Elves of the Reaches 2

Adrina, Emel, Vilmos, Galan and Seth must survive the greatest challenge Great Kingdom has faced in hundreds of years: the dissolution of the Kingdom Alliance and the battle to save Quashan'. Survival in a changing world depends on their ability to adapt and if they fail, their world and everything they believe in will perish.

THE KINGDOMS AND THE ELVES OF THE REACHES II

Keeper Martin's Tales

BOOK 2

ROBERT STANEK

THE KINGDOMS AND THE ELVES OF THE REACHES III

Keeper Martin's Tales

BOOK 3

ROBERT STANEK

The Kingdoms & the Elves of the Reaches 3 & 4

Adrina, Emel, Vilmos, Galan and Seth face even greater challenges as their world is transformed. Vilmos, in his quest to become the first human magus in a thousand years, must control the darkness within him. Adrina must accept her place and work together with Emel to help the elves make their plea to Great Kingdom's council. What happens along the way will amaze you.

THE KINGDOMS AND THE ELVES OF THE REACHES IV

Keeper Martin's Tales

BOOK 4

ROBERT STANEK

IN THE SERVICE OF DRAGONS

**The direct continuation of The Kingdoms &
the Elves of the Reaches!**

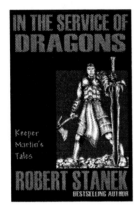
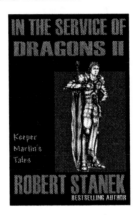

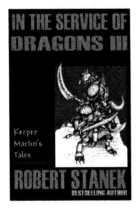
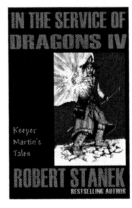

RUIN MIST TALES

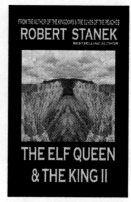

For every fantastic story you'll ever find there are often other stories that retell the adventures from different points of view—so why should it be any different in Ruin Mist? Join us now as we walk the dark path through the chronicles of Ruin Mist. Discover new secrets, new dangers, new visions and new realities!

MAGIC LANDS

Following the village elder's advice, Ray leaves his home village, setting out for the place lost and deep where he will find a companion for his journey to the stone land and where he will discover that there is no easy path from childhood to manhood. "Beware lashing tail and gnashing teeth," the village elder warns him, "and if Old Bull doesn't get you, Mother Slither surely will."

Printed in the United States
33587LVS00001B/7